CASCADE CRASH

Anthony W. Eichenlaub

oakleafbooks.com

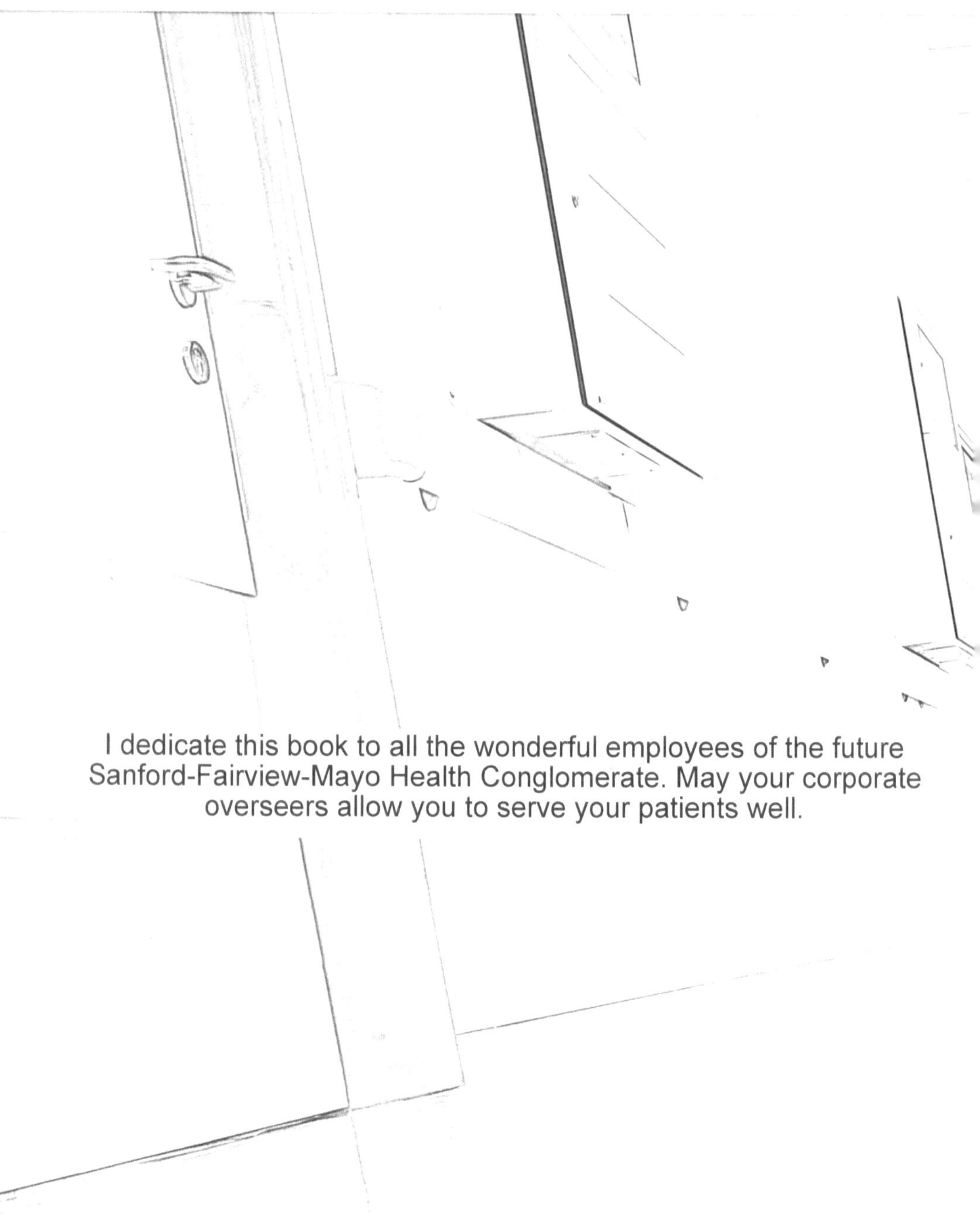

I dedicate this book to all the wonderful employees of the future Sanford-Fairview-Mayo Health Conglomerate. May your corporate overseers allow you to serve your patients well.

PART 1

THE CLINIC JOB

The O2 monitor beeped when everything was normal, and Ajay Andersen wondered if the thing would be even more annoying if and when things went south. He considered what he would do if he wanted to hack the device. It had a data port. It wouldn't be hard. Maybe he could reprogram it into silence.

But that would blow his cover.

He tugged at the bulky bracelet on his thin wrist. The device was IV insertion, O2 monitor, and blood pressure monitor all in one, and its stark, sterile white practically glowed against his brown skin. If he removed it, every frantic nurse within gasping distance would rush to his side.

This was, after all, the most prestigious, the most expensive, and the most difficult to infiltrate floor of the Sanford-Fairview-Mayo Clinic in Rochester, Minnesota.

Unfortunately, the bracelet interfered with his fidget—the holographic screen and motion-sensing set of rings that he used as a computing interface. He was going to need his full range of operation for what came next. He switched the rings to his right hand and gestured to activate the display over the back of his hand. Touching the hearing aid in his ear, he said, "I'm in."

"Proceed to phase two," said the voice on the other end. Maxwell Yeats wanted into the secure floor as badly as Ajay, and the man had all the skills Ajay didn't.

The SFM Clinic had always served elite patients. The old Dalai Lama had frequented the clinic, as had the young Tibetan Dalai Lama in recent years—many argued the Chinese-sponsored Dalai Lama didn't count anyway. Previous iterations of the clinic had served everyone from Lou Gehrig to President George H.W. Bush to Muhammad Ali. The recently remodeled top two floors of the ancient Mary Brigh building were designed for such celebrity patients.

And Ajay needed to visit the worst of the patients.

Randall Bent was an inventor and entrepreneur. A hero of capitalism hoisted to celebrity status by the sheer accumulation of wealth. His paranoia was legendary, and the security precautions surrounding his home estate were a work of genius.

Not even an old hacker like Ajay could hope to crack that. Not with the fall of encryption to quantum computing. Not with the newest, cleverest tech that Ajay had developed by his own hand. Not even with the help of his brilliant granddaughter, Kylie.

"Hey, Papa," Kylie said through their shared comm. He could tell by the fidelity of the connection that she was nearby, because Kylie was able to communicate wirelessly using a modification in her brain that Ajay had never quite understood.

"Hi, dear," he said, trying not to sound too tired. "Having fun?"

"This is town is *so* boring." Her tone shifted, and she whispered, "Did you get my flowers?"

Ajay looked at the yellow carnations. "They're perfect."

"Do you really think that guy can help?"

"We won't know until I talk to him."

"I'm going to take over Rochester's transit grid."

"Don't—"

The connection was gone.

The vase of carnations rocked when Ajay pulled himself to his feet and bumped the table. He caught it before it could topple to the floor. The card said it was from Kylie, and when he opened it, it played her favorite ultra-catchy synth-pop monstrosity. Sylvia Synth, Ajay thought. It was the worst music he'd ever heard.

He reached down around the flower stems and released a cache inside the vase.

Two tiny drones flew free. The music stopped.

Ajay closed his thin hospital gown—the kind that left little to the imagination and an uncomfortable breeze up his backside—and plucked his cane from the corner by the door. Kylie had built the cane for him, including everything from an integrated computing stack to a tip-mounted taser. His fidget connected wirelessly to a computer in the cane, giving him access to his best tools. He hung the cane on his IV tower so that he would have it nearby. The tower itself would need to come with him as he shuffled through the hospital.

The pod where they were keeping him was seven rooms arranged in a circle around the central nurse's station. It was the perfect setup, allowing only a few nurses to monitor the activities of every patient, but not ideal for Ajay's purpose. He preferred to *not* be monitored, thank you very much. He needed to send an alert so that Max could join him.

With a gesture, he sent the two tiny drones out on an exploration pattern.

That was when he glimpsed the men through the glass door between pods. Big, stupid slabs of meat—like livestock wandered in from a nearby field.

"We have a problem," Ajay hissed into his comm. "Bodyguards."

"We expected bodyguards," said Max.

"*A* bodyguard," said Ajay. "We expected one guy and we figured you could take him out without triggering a Code Red."

"Red?" Max asked. "Isn't that fire?"

The two men had shoulders like ancient oaks, and there wasn't half a neck to share between the two of them. Devices in their ears and on their eyes bristled with signals—these weren't some hired-off-the-street thugs. They were professionals.

One of them turned toward the glass door and stared directly at Ajay's drone. He sneered and the drone went careening back through Ajay's pod. It disappeared into a room on the opposite side of the circle from Ajay and crashed.

One of three nurses at the station perked up. He wore a thick beard and blue glasses. "Did you hear that?"

"I think you mean Code Green," said Max. "That's the one for violent behavior."

The bearded nurse rose to investigate the disturbance, and Ajay thought it looked like as good a distraction as he was going to manage. The other two nurses peered over the desk after their coworker.

"Green doesn't make any sense." Ajay swung the second drone around to monitor the nurse's station.

He dragged the IV stand behind him into the central pod desk. His heart slammed in his chest, making his bracelet flash a yellow warning. His years at the NSA had been spent behind a desk executing long-distance hacks on long-distance targets. The destruction of digital trust pushed hackers closer and closer to their targets.

In short, Ajay needed a better hobby. He drew a long breath to calm himself.

"What'd you find?" asked one of the nurses at the station. She was a tall woman with dark skin and short-cropped hair.

"Probably nothing," said the other. She was a plump woman with silver hair and creases at the corners of her eyes.

"Fire extinguisher," said the nurse in the room. Ajay breathed a sigh of thanks that she hadn't found the wrecked drone. "And some kind of drone." Crap.

The nurses at the desk were distracted, so Ajay spun the nearest screen around to face him and punched through a series of memorized commands. He worked fast and quiet, with the two nurses only a few paces from him. If he could execute the command without being spotted—

"Excuse me," said Nurse Beard, emerging from the room to see Ajay. "You can't be on that, sir." Polite and deferential, even in a reprimand. Ajay despised top-tier healthcare.

He typed faster.

"Excuse me!" the tall nurse nearest him said, more insistent than the bearded man. She spun the screen around and wrenched the keyboard from Ajay's grasp. He reached—failed. The final command was left unsent. "Mr. Andersen, I'm going to have to ask you to return to your room."

"I told you," said Ajay, "I need my pills."

"Maybe it's Code Orange," Max said over the comm.

"That's hazardous materials," Ajay snapped.

The tall nurse blinked. "Excuse me?"

"Not you," said Ajay. He needed to get into the other pod, and he needed a way to get past the two bodyguards. He tried to let an uncertain quaver enter his voice, which wasn't difficult. "I'm just confused."

"You have an IV," said the nurse. "All the medication you need right now is coming from that." He circled the desk and checked the machine on Ajay's wrist. "Everything's looking good, Mr. Andersen. The best thing for you right now is to return to your room and get some sleep."

Ajay returned to his room. He sat on the bed but didn't lie down.

All he needed to do was wait.

"White," said Max through the comm.

"What?"

"Code White. That's the one for violence."

"I thought that was for hemorrhage." Ajay sighed. "I suppose violence could cause that."

"Did you get the order sent or not?"

Ajay chewed his lower lip. "Almost."

"Almost? I thought you said you were the best, old man."

"Do you think it's from maintenance?" said the bearded nurse. It had taken him a few minutes to clean up the mess Ajay's hardware had made. She held the hand-sized drone up in front of her face and peered at its markings. Ajay watched her through the images collected by the second drone, which was now mounted on the ceiling and disguised as a sprinkler head. "Or do you think someone's really trying to spy on our patients?"

The nurses had the decency to look nervous. Their whole schtick was ultra-secure privacy. They were trained to recognize threats. This was very clearly a threat.

"We'll have to call it in," said the bearded man. "It's a violation."

The machine on Ajay's wrist buzzed. Meds coursed through his veins. He hadn't faked his way into the hospital. He really did need the surgery that he was in for. Cancer treatments were better than they ever had been, but the aggressive pancreatic cancer he was suffering from required the meds he was getting. The treatment was dangerous but fast-acting. Best in modern medicine.

He wasn't lying about the cancer, but he *was* lying about his identity. If the nurses triggered a full security audit, he'd be discovered, and he hadn't even gotten Max in the door yet. This would have been so much easier if the clinic allowed visitors in these pods.

There were a dozen networks in the pod, but only one controlled the phone systems. Ajay checked his permissions. The processes he'd set in place to crack that network were still churning away, slowly prying into the systems. He could make it faster, but that might reveal his attempts.

A good hacker took his time. A desperate hacker was fast. He swiped through the processes, fired three more cracking protocols, and delved into the code.

Alerts emerged almost immediately. Red waves of code washed over his holographic display, but he started a process to handle them. He caught the superficial alerts and shunted them to the null folder. Gone. With the extra time, he executed a fleet of obfuscating processes, designed to cover his tracks if anyone figured out he was there.

The nurse picked up the phone but was distracted by something Ajay couldn't see. Something in the direction of the glass door to the next pod. The pod where Ajay desperately needed to be.

"Maybe it's Code Black," Ajay said into the comm.

"Code Black is a bomb threat," said Max. "I can manage that if you think it might hurry things up a little."

"No need." Ajay dispersed a splash of orange warning text. The phone network evaded his capture, and he was running out of time. "I've got this." He totally didn't.

"A bomb threat would trigger the lockdown, anyway," Max admitted. "Same as the threat of violence."

Ajay found what he was looking for. A file with encryption keys floated unprotected in a temporary folder of the network filesystem. Jackpot. He grabbed the file and cracked it within a matter of seconds.

The nurse pushed a button on the phone. He was the only nurse at the station now, as the two women were checking on the other patients. Where were they? Ajay scoured the pod using the drone stuck to the ceiling.

His comm clicked, and Ajay said in his most professional voice, "Security."

"Yes, um, I think we have an incident." It was the bearded nurse at the station. "We found some kind of spy drone."

"Submit for a security audit. We'll send someone up immediately," Ajay said. He switched to Max's line. "That's your cue."

Maxwell arrived in the black uniform of Frontier Arms hired security staff. Frontier was the biggest mercenary corporation in Minnesota, and Ajay was pleased the man had the disguise available. Max had a gun at his hip, a bulky comm unit on his shoulder, and a pair of blue aviators covered in an augmented digital display. He wore a thin beard, and his long hair was pulled back in a neat ponytail.

"I'm going to need to search the whole floor," he said to the nurse. He pocketed the drone, and Ajay breathed a sigh of relief. The machine probably couldn't be traced back to him, but it wasn't a great idea to leave debris in his wake. "Please wait over here," he said, indicating one of the rooms.

"We need to be at the station," said Nurse Beard.

"I need to keep you safe." Max led two of the nurses into a room, plucked a broom from the nearby supply closet, and wedged it so that the door wouldn't open. Ajay briefly wondered where the third nurse went. The plump old lady was nowhere to be seen. Maybe she had gone on break.

The bodyguards, unfortunately, never went on break.

"All right, Ajay," Max said, eyeing the premium grade-A beef through the barrier between pods. "Two of them, two of us."

Ajay peered around the corner through the glass door. The two bodyguards still flanked the door to Randall Bent's room. They were huge. Even with luck and a cattle prod, Ajay didn't think he could take down one of them, and he didn't have either.

He eyed the cane hanging from his IV stand. Well, maybe he *did* have a cattle prod.

"That wasn't the deal," Ajay said. "You wanted in, I got you in."

"Plans change, old man."

"I was never a field agent."

"If you don't help, I'm going to have to shoot them both," said Max. He spoke as if it was an unfortunate detour on a long road trip.

"If you fire your gun, the alarms are going to trigger and the whole place will go into lockdown."

Ajay didn't like the hard set of Max's jaw. It was the cold, calculating expression of a shark. Sometimes Ajay had to work with unsavory people to get what he needed, and Max was no exception.

He stood from the bed, hospital gown flapping in the wind, and pulled his cane from where it still hung on his IV stand. The monitor on his wrist registered an increased heart rate as Ajay met Max's steely gaze. "Wait for my signal."

Ajay fingered the trigger on the end of his cane.

He walked like the old man he was, hunched over and tired, getting in a loop of exercise around the figure eight of the two connected circular pods. The glass doors opened for him, giving way to a facial recognition that he had programmed into the network. As soon as the door opened, the closest bodyguard turned and watched him.

It was a penetrating gaze. Deep and slick, like being watched by the Eye of Sauron. Ajay's cane clicked on the linoleum. The wheels of his IV stand wailed to protest their movement.

"Gentlemen," Max said to the bodyguards, stepping in behind Ajay. "We need to talk about a security breach."

The bodyguards didn't talk. They weren't the talking type. The farthest didn't move. He might have actually been a statue. The closest raked his icy gaze from Ajay to Max. Ajay's bracelet flashed yellow. They knew. They *had* to know.

"Nurses found something in the other pod," said Max. "Something we don't allow in a tight security setting like this."

The bodyguard's lips pressed tightly together. Ajay continued his slow, hobbled walk. He passed around the end of the nurse's station, listening to the chorus of beeps coming from the other rooms.

"Care to explain?" Max asked, holding out Ajay's drone. "This one of yours?"

The bodyguard looked at the drone, looked at Max, then looked at the drone again. "Nope." He was the one who had caused the drone to crash.

Ajay was halfway around the pod. The third nurse was nowhere to be seen, but a high-pitched alert sounded from one of the rooms. He stepped faster, dragging his IV stand.

Then, the second bodyguard moved. Somehow, even without a neck, he still managed to turn his square head to look at Max. It was the opportunity Ajay needed.

He took the cane up in two hands, lunged forward, and struck the bare skin at the base of the big man's skull.

Ajay's granddaughter Kylie loved arts and crafts. Over their years together, she had made him several things. A braided bracelet. A customized fidget. A cane with a taser on the end. She knew her business when it came to customized consumer tech.

A hundred thousand volts coursed through the man's skull. His mouth opened, his body tensed, and he dropped hard.

Max moved like lightning. He drew his taser and struck.

The bodyguard slapped Max's wrist and the taser flew across the pod—landing at the feet of the plump nurse. She stood outside a room with her mouth hanging open.

Shit.

The bodyguard struck Max in the neck and pounded him in the chest with a huge fist. The guard at Ajay's feet shook as if in seizure. Max reached for his gun.

Again, the bodyguard was too fast. He grabbed Max's arm and slammed him into the nurse's station.

The nurse went for the desk. She was going to trigger an alarm. Ajay stabbed his cane into the floor and activated his access wireless ports. The alert systems in this pod were separate from the one next to it, but he knew how to penetrate the system. He brought up the code as the nurse launched herself over the desk for the big emergency button. If she struck it, everything was done.

Max landed a powerful blow on the bodyguard's beefy face, but the big man didn't slow. Ajay found the override for the emergency button and redirected it as the nurse flung open the button's cover.

Got it. The button was useless when she pressed it.

Gunshots.

Max stood with his gun in an outstretched arm. The bodyguard staggered backward, gasping through a hole in his neck.

The nurse dropped to the floor.

All the lights turned red. Ajay swore. Lockdown. He stepped past the remaining bodyguard and pushed his way into Randall Bent's room just as the emergency barrier slammed into place, locking him in.

Quiet.

The room was dark and smelled of the heavy weight of sickness. Ajay pushed a curtain aside to see the long window looking out over the city. Assisi Heights stood on a hill not far away, looking like a castle defending the town against the cool Minnesota night. A shadow moved in the room. Randall Bent's emaciated form shifted in his bed.

And next to him on the side table lay the data brick.

In his view through his drone, Ajay saw the burn of red lights and the flash of more gunfire. A shape moved before the glass door—the bodyguard he had stunned was on the move.

Ajay moved across the room. There in the quiet of the protected hospital room, nothing of the chaos outside seeped in through the lockdown doors. The wealthy man lived as he always had—fully secluded from the madness of the world he helped create.

And Ajay despised him for it.

His cane's universal connector clicked into place, then the encrypted data stream flowed laser-sharp across his holographic display. It was a flow of nonsense designed to waste the time of hackers. The real data lay beneath, on a communication layer accessible only using an antiquated token ring handshake. Ajay executed the sequence, and the communication flow started. His tip had been correct.

The original plan had been to steal the data brick, but Max had been certain it would self-destruct if moved too far away from Randall. Ajay didn't doubt the man, who was still wrestling the bodyguard. The gun was nowhere to be seen. Gone in the struggle. The two crashed into the nurse's station, toppling over.

The nurse scrambled away, and Ajay breathed a sigh of relief. She had survived. So far, anyway.

"Hurry up," Max hissed into the comm.

Ajay blinked. The data connection was complete, but how had Randall organized his information? It wasn't alphabetical or by timestamp. Rows of folders spread across a wide open plain like poppies in a field. How would he find one particular piece of information? His data connection wasn't fast enough to copy it all. That would take weeks.

"You're my first visitor," rasped Randall.

Ajay looked to see the man's big eyes staring at him in the filtered moonlight. Awake, the man's vitality shone through his otherwise gaunt features. His dark skin and high cheekbones made him look elfin, and his mop of gray hair gave him almost a boyish look.

"I've bought and sold cities, you know," Randall said. "But no money will purchase the love of a family."

Ajay swiped through the data feed and searched for each of Randall's seven children. Nothing. "They only stay away because they don't want to cause you stress."

"They don't want to cause *themselves* stress." Randall raised his left arm, which held a bracelet much like the one that tethered Ajay to the IV stand. "Wait till they understand how this works."

A Vitalink. Ajay said, "If you die, the data brick is toast. What about a backup?"

"*When* I die," Randall said. "And I killed the backup before I came here."

In the nurse's pod, the bodyguard pounded Max's face against a shattered screen. It wasn't going well. The security response team could arrive in seconds, and Ajay was no closer to finding Randall's secrets. This was supposed to have been a much quieter operation.

"You're here to die," said Ajay.

Randall closed his eyes and leaned his head back, drawing a long, slow breath. "People don't come to the greatest medical institution in the hemisphere to die."

"You do." Ajay started a procedure to find the newest files on the data brick. Medical data. He saw scans of the cancer infecting Randall's body. Aggressive. Deadly. There were some cancers even modern medicine couldn't cure. "You're here because you are no longer safe at home."

Randall's eyes snapped open. "There is no such thing as safe."

Ajay envisioned the man's wretched life. He was a victim of his own wealth, paranoid beyond belief, unable to ever trust a single soul with his secrets. To even the barest shred of his wealth.

"How long have you been alone?" Ajay asked.

"Twenty-five years have passed since the pandemics. My cures were supposed to make the world a better place, but how could I give them away for free? I couldn't get the research completed without funding. I couldn't get funding without the backing of big pharma."

"And the pharmaceutical companies demanded patents."

"And profits," the old man spat. "They sold their cure to the wealthiest of the wealthy. As people died in their squalid homes, the rich lived without risk."

"You profited, too," Ajay said as he scoured the brick for the dates of the pandemics. The patents were all there, but important details were missing. "Where is it?"

"Trevan Pharmaceuticals took half of my patents," the old man spat. "The rest—" He fell into a fit of coughing.

Trevan. It was the corporation responsible for human experimentation. It was Trevan where Kylie was born and lived the first half of her life.

In the video feed, Ajay saw Max land a powerful kick on the bodyguard. The gun was almost within reach, but when Max dove for it, the bodyguard took advantage of the distraction to dive behind cover. Max swore over the comm.

"Who?" Ajay grabbed the older man's shoulder. "Who has the rest of your tech?"

Randall swallowed with a dry click. His breaths were coming ragged and harsh. "It's too late." He held up his wrist with the Vitalink. "It's too late."

"You're not dead yet, Randall," Ajay said. He leaned in close so that he was sure the man could see the determination in his eyes. "I have a granddaughter. She's just a kid, but there's something special about her. She needs what you have. Your patents. Your data."

A pained smile crossed Randall's face, and a tear hung on the precipice of falling. "I only wish I could have helped."

"You can!" Ajay shouted. "This *one* thing. Just this once. Tell me where I can find the rest of your data."

In the pod, Max fired two more shots, but the bodyguard was nowhere to be seen. Overhead, a voice called a Code White.

"Code White!" Max shouted.

"Thanks, asshole," Ajay muttered into the comm.

"It's not in the patents," Randall said. "Patents become public. What we made was a method of repairing neurological damage. Anybody worth anything would spend everything for something like that if they needed it." He coughed and spat a lump of phlegm. "Everything."

Ajay used keywords to search Randall's data but came with nothing but blank files. "Who has it?"

"Ajay," Max shouted. "I need to get out of here!"

"Orin Instruments," Randall whispered.

"The fitness tracker company?" Ajay asked. He searched the brick and downloaded everything with the company's tag.

"Biomed is biomed," Randall said. "Profit is profit."

"They kept your ideas."

"Hoarded them. Used them and refused to ever let them help those who really needed it."

Ajay had a hard time feeling bad for the man. He could have spilled his secrets at any time but chose not to for fear of losing his wealth.

"I have what we need," Ajay said into the comm. To Randall, he said, "You've done a good thing today, old man. This will help me. It'll help my daughter. When I'm done, your secrets will be where anyone can find them."

After a second's hesitation, a slip of a smile crossed Randall's face. "They never solved the Cascade. It's the one secret I kept."

"What is the Cascade?"

The dying man chuckled to himself.

Ajay leaned down so he was inches from the man's bony face. "Tell me!"

The sack of bones only laughed. His laughter dissolved into a hacking cough. Ajay would need to learn about it from the data he had taken from the data brick.

With the blast doors down, Ajay was trapped. Max was trapped. Security would arrive, and they'd all be stuck with their hands in the cookie jar.

Ajay looked at the sensor on his wrist. Blood pressure. IV. Pulse. Oxygen.

He expelled his air and held his breath. Seconds passed. In his video feed, he watched Max shoot the bodyguard in the chest. The bodyguard touched the wound, and his hands came away covered in blood.

"These guys are the worst of the worst, Ajay," said Max, as if sensing Ajay's silent protest. "It's hard to feel bad for killing these two."

It still didn't settle well with Ajay, but there was nothing he could do. He continued to hold his breath, clamping around his neck with one hand to keep from giving in. His bracelet flashed yellow, then red. It blinked several times and its inside band engaged a full sensor sequence for a more accurate reading.

Then it flashed a full alert. It was connected to the nurse's computers, which were connected to the emergency blast doors. Code White was a big deal, but no medical institution would allow an emergency protocol that would prevent them from attending to a patient in need.

The door slid open.

Max stepped into the room. He raised his gun, pointing it at Randall Bent. His glasses were now gone, and a rough wound crossed the bridge of his nose.

Ajay stepped between him and the old man, raising his hands. "Let him go in peace, Max."

Max didn't blink. "You know I can't do that, Ajay."

"We have what we're here for," said Ajay. "The mission's done."

"*You* have what you're here for." Max stepped to the side, but Ajay matched the movement. "I'm here to kill the man whose greed killed my family."

Then it all made sense. The hard look in Max's eyes. The information he had on the wealthy Randall Bent. The way he had found Ajay on the forums and attracted him to the project with hints of the secrets Randall held—without explaining what Max himself would get for it beyond the modest paycheck. Ajay had been a fool for following along, but if he had known, would he have done anything differently? He needed the information that Randall would have taken to his grave.

Ajay touched the controls on his cane, retracting his universal connector. Using its holographic display, he showed the medical imagery of the dying man. "Murder is no way to honor the dead," he said.

Max pointed his gun at Ajay's face. "Move."

"He's suffering," Ajay said. "He's suffering and he's going to die alone in this dark room, separated by a quarter century from anyone he might have ever loved. You lost people? Well, he lost people, too."

Max's hand shook. His eyes were sunken. He stared at Ajay and his expression became a tortured mix of pain and anger and hate.

And then, he broke. With a scream, he shoved Ajay to the side and fired into Randall Bent's chest. Then, his aim flicked to the side, and he fired again. The window popped at the first shot, and several more shots spiderwebbed the thick glass. He kicked out the window.

Lights from a car-sized drone shone from above, and Max climbed onto the windowsill and hooked a rope to his belt.

"Are you coming?" he shouted over the roar of the blades.

Ajay stared out the window. His brain couldn't grasp what Max had just done. He wasn't supposed to leave this way. The plan had been for Ajay to retire to his own room, but the plan also hadn't involved the killing of two bodyguards. If he fled now, he could avoid any problems. He wouldn't need to deal with the aftermath of their destruction.

In the pod outside, he heard hard boots and the shouts of security personnel.

He said, "I'll be in touch."

Max leaped from the window and grasped the drone. He pulled himself inside its small compartment and flew away into the night.

Ajay plastered a look of abject fear on his face just before the first armed security guard entered the room. He raised his hands and even managed to squeeze a tear out of one eye. "He went that way," he said, pointing out the window.

The guy lowered his weapon. Moments later, the security lockdown was lifted. Ajay made his way back to his room, careful not to roll his IV stand through the pools of blood or over the shattered glass. He settled back onto his bed and forced himself to breathe.

Then, he remembered the nurse. She hadn't seen him, had she? He tried to remember the exact moment she had emerged from the room. His heart pounded in his chest. He hurt. Everything hurt. Nausea rolled through his gut with the adrenaline crash and his bracelet pulsed with red.

The old nurse came in, summoned by the bracelet. She took his other arm, checked his rapid pulse, and clicked her tongue. "I'm sorry about the excitement, Mr. Andersen," she said. "We'll be moving everyone to another pod very soon."

He stared at her for several seconds before answering. "Thank you."

Before she left, she leaned in close and whispered, "You'll make the cure public?"

Ajay blinked. "You heard everything?"

A smile twinkled in her eyes. "The acoustics are really something in these newer pods."

Ajay's heart finally settled and the disquiet in his bones eased. It wasn't always apparent, and he couldn't always count on them, but there were allies everywhere for what he did. As long as he could fight, he'd fight for them. As long as there was truth to be found, he'd find it.

"Thank you," he whispered as the nurse left the room. She paused without turning, nodded, and then continued on her way to check the remaining patients.

PART 2

HACKER ON THE CHICAGO EXPRESS

Ajay Andersen elbowed his way through the stifling crowd of Union Depot in Minneapolis as the last boarding call echoed through the vast building. His cane clacked on the polished marble floor, and well-dressed businessmen muttered curses under their breath when he swiped them aside with a mean scowl and a wave of his knobby-knuckled hand. He passed the towering columns and restaurants that smelled of bitter coffee and freshly baked scones. His old knees protested as he delved deep into the tunnels of the depot.

The message he received had been clear: get on the train now or miss the opportunity.

Then, he was there. The silver slug of a train sat before him like a bullet polished to a perfect shine. He flashed a holographic image—the one he had just acquired through dubious means—and boarded the Chicago Express.

"Two hours," said an old man as Ajay settled in next to him. "Amazing what they can do these days, isn't it?"

"Two hours," Ajay agreed. Two hours before the train arrived in Chicago. Two hours to hack the train's integrated security. Two hours to find Remy Larrimer, rob him of his precious cargo, and escape into the void. "Sometimes I feel like it would be better if trains weren't so fast."

He slipped a pair of half-moon cheaters on the bridge of his nose and paired them with the fidget interface on his left hand.

"You an Indian?" asked the old man next to him.

Ajay bristled with annoyance. He *was* Indian, but not the way the man thought. His father was from the Delhi region in northern India. His mother's side of the family was Norwegian but had more generations in Minnesota than he had ever bothered to count. The mix made sure he didn't fully fit in wherever he went, and it tended to confuse idiots. To the old man, all he said was, "Something like that."

The man humphed.

It took Ajay twenty-five seconds to hack into the train's network, disable the countermeasures, and bring up a registry of the train's passengers. It wasn't a record. Long ago when he had worked for the NSA, he would have been able to do the same in ten, but those were the days when encryption ruled the internet and passwords were the names of pets. Things were harder in modern times. Security was a game of smoke and mirrors.

"Computer guy, eh?" said the man next to him, taking another ill-advised tack at conversation. He wore a gray fedora and a button-down shirt. Fancy for the lower level of the cheapest passenger car.

"You could say that."

"Big plans in Chicago?"

"It's more about the journey," Ajay said. It was, too. Once in Chicago, he was planning on turning around and returning to Minnesota.

The old man jabbered on, but Ajay tuned him out with a few quick commands to his hearing aid. Rude, maybe, but he needed to concentrate. Eventually, the man stopped trying to force the conversation.

The Chicago Express wasn't a long train. It ran hot and fast, with seven cars for passengers, seven for cargo, and a final launch car in the caboose. Ajay swiped through the manifest of each car, searching for his target. Each registry came up short.

Because this was the wrong list. Ajay cursed himself. He'd fallen for a honey pot—an easy target set out as a decoy for lazy hackers.

The door in the front of his car opened, and a man in dark sunglasses entered. He had a narrow face, calloused knuckles, and tight lips pressed into a perpetual scowl.

"Conductor," said the old man next to Ajay. "Hope your ticket's good."

Ajay's ticket wasn't good. "It'll be fine." He touched the controls on the top of his cane and flashed through the manifest again. He had searched for the one name he knew to verify the list. His own. But now that he looked on the network, there were a hundred lists that contained him. A thousand. This was security through obscurity—the laziest of all defenses. If he wanted to find the whole list, he was going to need to know more names.

And the honey pot had already alerted security.

Ajay stood from his seat and made his way back toward the stairs.

Outside of the window, the Mississippi River raced past on one side and the quaint town of Red Wing on the other. They'd already gone over fifty miles. He needed to hurry up and find Remy Larrimer.

His heart pounded as he ascended the stairs. The passenger car closest to the rear was a sardine can of humanity, cramming three layers of people where the other cars only had two. He pushed through the narrow row and cast glances back toward the huddled masses.

Jackie Green, Percival Lorentz, Wendy Kohl. Facial recognition in his cheaters tagged name after name. He used that information to find lists on the network, then cross-referenced that list with the ones containing his name.

"Excuse me," said the conductor, calling out to Ajay. Crap.

Then he had it. The real list. And there, in the upper level of the second passenger car, sat the man he was after: Remy Larrimer, heir to the Larrimer estate, copper-nickel mining tycoon, crypto trillionaire until the fall of encryption, and, if every rumor swirling around the potential political candidate were to be believed, all-around asshole.

Ajay was going to rob the man blind.

"Sir," said the conductor, closing the distance.

Ajay needed to move. His access to the internal network didn't give him control over the train, but it let him control some of the internal systems. He hit the lights, flashed an alert message across the feed, and ran.

The chaos was instantaneous. Passengers cried out as the lights went black. The windows still shone their tinted sunlight, but the shifting light gave the train an eerie look. Then, alerts flashed on people's devices. Floods. Fires. Tornadoes.

By the time Ajay hit the door in the front of the car, the conductor was being swarmed.

Ajay crashed through the gate and into a roaring cacophony between cars. It was an airtight space, but it wasn't an area meant for passengers. Ajay pushed through and down into the lower level of the sixth car.

This car wasn't as packed. It held families on their way for a weekend jaunt and mid-tier businessmen on their way to the bigger city. He rushed past them, his heart pounding. When he saw an empty seat, he sat in it.

The conductor rushed past and pushed through to the forward train.

When, finally, Ajay's breathing slowed, he slipped his cheaters back on and checked the manifest one more time. Larrimer was there. He was sure of it.

But the front three passenger cars were heavily guarded. Guarded and secure. Ajay's old hands shook as he worked his way into the systems.

The train's network was surprisingly secure. In its outer layer, Ajay could access information, like the manifest, but even there, measures had been taken to hide the most valuable data. He used his access to search the file system, checking little-known directories for hints about key locations.

There were millions. An overwhelming amount of wrong information was apparently a favorite method of obfuscation for whoever ran the train's network. Fine, Ajay thought, we can work with that. Using the true manifest, he found links to the correct version of the keyfile. From there, he found new access. Not root-level access, but a more secure operational level.

Which meant cameras.

This had to be perfect. He had only one chance at this, and he hadn't had enough time to prepare. The information he'd received had been late, giving him only minutes to board the train, and now he was working alone against all the security of one of the richest men in Minnesota.

But if he could get Larrimer's ring, he could take a significant chunk of the man's fortune. With that, he could fund the mission that would save his granddaughter. His amazing, brilliant, granddaughter.

Ironically, she would be able to handle all of this. Kylie swam through code like a crocodile through water. She was special, born with technology in her head that gave her the ability to communicate directly with machines as if it were her first native language. Maybe it was. The only problem was the Cascade: a devastating problem with the technology that had killed too many other enhanced children.

Unfortunately, Ajay didn't know enough about the Cascade to help his granddaughter. Orin Instruments had taken everything the inventor had discovered and hidden it behind a firewall. To get it, Ajay would need allies. To get allies, Ajay needed money.

Kylie would have a solution to his problem on the train. The girl would take one look at the network, crack it wide open, and—

What?

Kylie's ability didn't just let her communicate with machines. It let her manipulate her own brain in interesting ways. She could change her temperament, calm herself, and dampen her emotions. Kylie could *be* anyone she wanted. It was part blessing and part curse.

Then, Ajay had an idea.

"Welcome to Wisconsin," intoned a voice from above. The shores of the Mississippi faded away behind them as the train sped through the deciduous forest. Time was running short.

Ajay brought up the manifest again, this time checking the cargo cars, following the data links through the lists of cargo to find what he needed. When he found it, he wrote a tracking program so that he knew where the conductor was.

There, one car over, the conductor confronted a pair of teens. Good. That would keep him busy.

Ajay moved back through the train, past the chaos of the seventh car. The alerts had stopped, and the lights were back on, but the residents of the cheapest car were on edge. They'd been packed in so tight that their body odor filled the space as the train rattled forward on its tracks.

The old man stepped in front of Ajay as he made his way down the aisle. There was suspicion in the man's eyes as he pointed a knobby finger at Ajay's chest. "It was this guy," he said. "Mr. Computer."

The crowd rumbled disapproval. Ajay's cheaters flashed. The conductor approached.

"I don't know what you're talking about," Ajay said. He tried to push past the old man, but a bony hand gripped his arm.

"I saw what you're up to," the old man hissed. "You're some kinda hacker."

Ajay wrenched his arm away and left for the baggage cars. The door slammed shut as the conductor entered the last passenger car.

Bernie Sorensen. That was the old man's name, according to the manifest. Ajay filed that away for later and pushed through baggage.

Racks of luggage towered above him, secured to the sides and barely contained in rattling cages. He raced through that car into the next and the next. Finally, in the second to last car, Ajay found what he needed: spare uniforms for the train staff.

He tried to remember the conductor's outfit. A crisp suit, with red borders along the cuffs and lapels. A nametag. The quintessential conductor's hat. He found spares for each except for the tablet computer the man had carried. That, he would need to fake.

Or.

His mind raced. He didn't have anything against the conductor. It wasn't like the man deserved a hard time for trying to maintain order on his train. But Ajay needed that tablet. The screen would have a hardware key for the more secure cars.

Ajay tried the next cargo car but found that it didn't have spare computing equipment at all. It held the nicest drone car he had ever seen. It was sleek silver and gold, with folded rotors tucked tight against its aerodynamic frame. The black tinted glass of its windshield shone in the dark space of the cargo hold, and two spotlights mounted on its front resembled staring white eyes.

Beyond that, there was nothing. A single window showed the tracks as they disappeared into the distance. They were already halfway through Wisconsin, and the tracks sped into the distance faster than ever.

Ajay connected to the train's surveillance. He needed that tablet, and for that, he needed to find the conductor.

Luckily, that wasn't going to be a problem. The conductor entered the first cargo car, tablet slung from a strap around his shoulder and a taser in one hand. Each wary step took him closer to Ajay—closer to the intruder he sought.

Ajay pushed his way forward, weighing his options as he moved. He could fight. The chances of Ajay, an old man, beating the young and healthy conductor didn't seem likely. He could use the taser mounted in his cane. That might take the man down quickly enough. He could try to sneak past—trust his hacking skills to crack the secure car's door.

Or, he could talk. "I'm glad you came," Ajay said, stepping into the first cargo car. Luggage cages rattled as the train sped along the tracks. "We need to chat."

The conductor gripped a taser in his left hand. "Mr. Ajay Andersen," he said. "Fella back there says you're the one hacking the train's systems."

"Bernie Sorensen?" Ajay asked. "We go way back. No, he's just messing with you."

The conductor narrowed his eyes. "You're in a restricted area." The taser crackled in his grip. "I'm going to have to restrain you until we arrive. After that, the police—"

"I don't think you want to do that." Ajay made his way to the center of the car. He was only a lunge away from the conductor, but he still didn't like his odds.

"You're dressed like me. I see what you're doing, sir. It's not going to work."

"You're right," Ajay said. "It won't work without that tablet. That's the key, isn't it?"

"Sir, if you could—"

"I'd rather not."

The conductor reached for Ajay's arm, but Ajay was ready for it. He stepped back and swung the heavy head of his cane. It missed the man by a mile and rattled the cage next to them.

The clasp holding the cage shut broke, and the door slid open. As the train rounded a long bend, luggage slid toward the now-unprotected aisle. The conductor moved to close the gate, and Ajay pushed past, lifted the man's tablet, and ran.

On his way past, Ajay connected to the door's lock and overrode the emergency release. It should stay closed for several minutes—hopefully, enough time for Ajay to—

"At it again, huh?" sneered Bernie Sorensen.

Ajay turned slowly. The old man watched him from the open door into the last passenger car. "Let me pass, Bernie."

"Bernie, is it?" said the old man. "Tryin' to impress me by figurin' out my name? I'm not some stooge for you, hacker. I know how you people work."

Ajay bristled. He was close to reaching the private car and this old idiot was going to get in his way. He couldn't explain to this man that he worked for the betterment of common people. He didn't steal from normal working-class folks just to line his pockets. Ajay stole from the wealthy. The *extremely* wealthy.

He did it to line his pockets, but still. There was some nuance there.

Either way, he didn't have time for such nuance. He flung a couple of data-scrapers at Bernie's identity and strolled forward with his jaw hard and his fists clenched.

Then, he said, "Bernie Sorensen, I don't mean any harm to you. I don't care if you've worked for the city of Chicago as a law clerk for nearly forty years. I don't care that you've always had two cats, ever since the day you first graduated from college. I don't care that five years ago someone stole your identity and ruined your already rough credit score. I don't care that your mother died of cancer or your wife left you for a baseball player. It doesn't matter to me that you had too much to drink on a warm night three summers ago and ended up starting a fire that consumed three homes."

"It—it was an accident," sputtered the old man.

"None of that matters to me." With every revelation, Ajay took another step closer until his breath danced across the old man's mustache. "What matters to me right now is that there is a man in this train who *deserves* what's coming for him. Right here." He thumped his cane on the floor. "Right now. You're going to let me pass because if you don't, you'll going to find out what it's like to be on the wrong side of the best hacker ever to grace the manure fire we call a network."

Bernie's lower jaw worked, but he said nothing.

"Step aside, Bernie."

Bernie stepped aside. "You won't fool anyone," he said as Ajay stepped past. "You don't look anything like the conductor."

"I don't have to," said Ajay.

Ajay stopped when he reached the entryway to the second story of the private car. This, according to the manifest, was the most likely place he would find Remy Larrimer. He drew a deep breath and calmed himself. Bernie was right. Nobody would believe that he was the conductor. His best option was to stay out of sight. Step into the private car as if he were conducting a routine operation, get what he needed, and then leave.

He pushed a button on the tablet's screen, and the door opened to a wall of muscle.

The giant wore a three-piece suit, bowler hat, and leather gloves. A bulge showed a holster under his breast pocket and the cold expression in his eyes said he meant business. What worried Ajay, though, were the man's shoes. He wore boots. Not cowboy boots or work boots, but heavy shit-kicker military boots.

So much for sneaking in unnoticed.

"Who is it, Junior?" asked a voice from inside the private car.

The big man's lip twisted. "It's the conductor."

Ajay swallowed his doubt and did his best impression of a servant. "Just here for a routine check, sir."

"Let him in," said the voice. The big man stepped aside.

Remy Larrimer's personal car was larger than almost every apartment Ajay had lived in during his career in the NSA. It sported a retrofuturistic style, with a stainless steel bar, plush velvet seating, and a rounded white ceiling. A row of framed data components lined the wall above a plush sofa. He felt like he had stepped into a rocket ship from the Fifties, but it was a rocket ship with an open bar and a dozen screens.

"Ah, the conductor," said a heavyset man bellied up to the bar. Remy Larrimer himself. A well-cut bartender poured top-shelf liquor into a shaker. "Thanks, Junior."

The man sputtered, "It's—"

"I know who it is, son. He's here to rob me."

Ajay straightened his back and summoned all the dignity he could muster. His mind raced with the possibilities. What had happened? Had he gotten a bad tip? No, that doesn't seem right. He had needed to rush to make the train, but he'd vetted the data. He'd covered his tracks. How would Remy know who he was?

As far as Ajay could see, he didn't have any good moves left, so he played a bad one. "I still expect to be paid."

"What?" said Junior.

"I have the contract right here," said Ajay. He clicked through the holographic interface on his cane, opening a comm channel to his granddaughter. "Somewhere."

Junior said, "Watch it, old man."

"No, no, I have it," Ajay said to Remy. "The deal was to steal your ring, and it's signed by your son. All above board, of course. White hat hacking's a good business to be in these days, but I'm afraid I didn't find many security flaws in your setup, even in transit like this." Ajay gestured at the older man's hand. "That ring, right there, with the crypto crystal."

Remy shot his son an expression so cold it risked freezing his son's sour face.

"I don't know what he's talking about," said Junior.

To Ajay, Remy said, "Drink?"

"Don't mind if I do." Ajay moved to the bar as the bartender mixed him something that smelled of pineapple and rum. The bartender's face might have been carved from marble when he finally pushed the drink across the bar to Ajay.

"White hat, you say?" said Remy, settling into one of the U-shaped chairs.

"Let's go with gray," said Ajay. "Mostly beneficial, with a side of light skullduggery."

Remy chuckled at that. "And my son hired you?"

Ajay flicked through the interface on his cane again, but this time he found the contract right away. It sat in a message from Kylie. He enlarged the message so that Remy could look, but hopefully not large enough that he could see that the contract was assembled by a frantic fourteen-year-old girl. "You have a smart son, Mr. Larrimer. Takes initiative to hire a security audit like this."

Junior sputtered, "I didn't—"

"Can it, Junior," snapped Remy. "The adults are talking."

Junior seethed but didn't protest any further. He deposited his massive, muscled body on the sofa under the row of old crypto wallets.

"Indeed," said Remy. The politician didn't give away anything in his expression. If he believed the contract, did he think his son was stealing from him? Ajay hoped so. It made his chance of survival marginally stronger.

The train wailed as it started to slow. Outside, the first sprawl of Chicago suburbs started to decorate the terrain. He was running out of time.

Junior glared daggers at Ajay.

Remy shook his head. "Don't mind my boy's suspicious nature."

"He's not out of line," Ajay said.

"And I don't care." He waved the ring in front of his face. "As far as everyone knows, I lost everything in the fall of crypto, but I was one of the first adopters of growth crystal. I wear the products of my wealth now."

Ajay gestured at the train car. "You don't appear to be doing too poorly." He pretended to take a sip of his drink, then pretended to appreciate it. It smelled awful.

Remy leaned forward to whisper, "Tell that to my son. He has grand plans, you know. For the family."

"Plans that don't involve your political career?" Ajay forced himself to breathe slowly. The offer had to be clear but not overt. "Or maybe he would rather hire a gray hat hacker to do security audits on your rivals."

Greed flashed in the man's eyes. "Can you do that?"

"Can I? I can do that now, sitting right here. Cryptography is broken, but believe me, people still air their dirty laundry online."

"What would you charge for something like that?"

Ajay said, "How much did you say that ring was worth?"

"This thing's worth more secrets than there are in Washington."

Junior crossed the room and grabbed Ajay by the arm in a bruising grip. "He's lying, Father. There's nothing this asshole can give you."

"You hired him, son," said Remy. "You're telling me he's not trustworthy?"

Junior twitched at the loaded question. Ajay could practically smell the gears turning in the big guy's head.

Remy slipped the ring from his finger and placed it on the bar. "It's yours if you can tell me what Travis Hogarth does with his Saturday evenings."

"Hogarth?" The old man wanted info on his political rival. Not very creative, but it was something Ajay could easily provide. Ajay slipped his half-moon cheaters onto the bridge of his nose and activated the network through his cane.

The thing about code is that non-coders often treated it like magic. The text flying across the holographic screen wasn't even complex. It wasn't dangerous or subversive. It was a simple route through the train's local network. A security hack that found the conductor and tracked him. Next, Ajay did as Remy had asked. He searched on the network for connections to Travis Hogarth.

But that wasn't all he did. He also, in the screen formed by the left lens of his cheaters, started to program his drone. The little device dropped from his cane to the floor and quietly floated under the shiny metal bar.

Junior breathed down his neck, watching the text flying across his holographic display.

"The best way to find the information people want hidden is to poke and prod until you find a counterattack," Ajay explained.

Junior grunted as if he understood the strategy.

Seconds passed. Then minutes. The Chicago skyline zoomed past, and their train ran alongside another, racing to their destination.

Then, there it was. Red swaths of text spilled like blood across his screen. Warnings flared and he took the streams of data and redirected them into sandboxes where they could spin harmlessly. Sweat beaded on his brow. He hadn't expected this to get so dicey so fast, but he ran with it. An array of obfuscators sought to muddy the data in Hogarth's mainframe, but Ajay knew what he was looking for.

The AI-generated false information all came with a marker, which the antiquated system used to sort the good data from the bad. Travis Hogarth wanted the world to believe that he was a saint. He spent Saturday evenings helping out at shelters or playing games with his family. The records all agreed that Hogarth was a kind, gentle man who only wanted the best for the state he represented.

But that couldn't have been further from the truth.

Politicians *wanted* a surveillance state. They all pushed for it. Worst of all were the politicians who fought for freedom and independence. They offered a false promise of freedom through policing and policing through surveillance.

It was a universal truth that those who pushed hardest for ubiquitous surveillance wanted to be surveilled the least.

Ajay swiped and sent a series of videos to the train's screen. His holographic display flickered, but nothing happened.

"Um," said Ajay, "I need access to your screens."

Remy's eyes narrowed, but he said, "Grant it."

"What?" Junior protested.

"Do it," Remy growled.

Junior grudgingly punched a code into the machines, and the screens came alive. Ajay swiped again, and a video emerged on the largest panel. Travis Hogarth, clearly recognizable even without the facial recognition tag floating over his head, entered the gambling hall of the notorious Treasure Island Casino. Overhead cameras didn't show him. He had been scrubbed from those.

But personal devices picked him up just fine, and Ajay switched from one video feed to the next as people operated their phones in the busy space. Hogarth moved through the crowd, spoke with the staff, and then met with a man.

"That," Ajay said, "is Cullins, a crime boss. He's a human trafficker and Canadian smuggler."

Remy watched the video as it played out on the big screen. Cullins, a greasy lump of a human being, spoke behind closed doors with Travis Hogarth. Ajay only had snippets of the two together, but it was clear that there was some kind of deal going down.

"This took you ten minutes," Remy said.

"Your son only hires the best."

That got a grunt of approval from the old man and a glare from Junior. Ajay reached for the ring, but Remy grabbed his wrist.

"Not so fast," said the politician. "How do I know it's true?"

"You think I deep faked it?" Ajay asked. "In ten minutes?"

"It could have been footage you stored somewhere," said Junior. "Because you knew what we'd ask."

Ajay pulled his wrist away from Remy. "You think that I guessed what you would ask on the off chance that you captured but didn't kill me? Now you really must think I'm a genius."

"We'll check it out," said Remy.

"I want my payment," said Ajay.

This time, father and son worked together. Junior grabbed him by the shoulders and shoved him to the door.

Remy followed. "We'll check it out," he repeated. "And you'll get your payment if it's good."

Ajay struggled. "We had a deal, Larrimer." He pushed back against Junior, but the big guy manhandled him, shoving him to the ground. Ajay picked up his cane, struggled to his feet, and glared at the two.

Junior slammed him against the wall with bruising force.

"Wait," Ajay gasped. His cane had an integrated taser. He could maybe hit Junior. Maybe. "Wait, I'm sorry. I'll go."

Remy placed a hand on his son's arm, holding him back. Ajay struggled to stay on his feet, taking a moment to gather his strength. Hitting the wall had hurt, and he wanted to be able to walk when he stepped out of that door.

He also needed to buy more time.

Grasping his cane, he stood as tall and proud as he could. Ajay had never much been one to bow before authority, and he had never respected the authority of wealth. Remy, a politician, ought to have commanded some shred of respect, but the way the man bandied about his wealth and power left Ajay disdainful of the old shit.

"We're even, then," said Ajay.

"Get out of here," said Remy. "And be thankful for the whiskey you drank."

The door behind him opened, and Ajay took a step through it. The doorway perfectly framed the politician and his son. Behind them, Ajay saw the screens still playing surveillance footage of Hogarth, and the bar still held the shining ring. Ajay doubted the ring was worth as much as the old man said. It was money. That was true.

But money was not the greatest wealth in the world.

Ajay's tiny drone slipped through the crack as the door closed. He caught it in the palm of his hand, slipped the old data chip from its grasp, and slotted the drone back into his cane.

"Now," he whispered into the command module of his cane.

Even through the door, the volume hurt Ajay's ears. Every device the Larrimers owned—everything in their massive private train car—blasted at full volume. He had the screens show a montage of the sins of father and son, from the time Remy had paid off the Minnesota Secretary of State to fix an election to the time Junior had met with a crime boss named Cullins in the Treasure Island Casino.

Then, Ajay ran. The data stream he carried spread through the train as he moved, playing on every device of every passenger. As the train slowed along the outskirts of Chicago, every passenger was treated to images of young Remy cheating on his wife and hiring an underaged prostitute. Audio played of Junior beating homeless people to death in the streets of Minneapolis.

As Ajay passed into the next car, he heard Junior burst in after him. "I'm gonna kill you, old man!"

His timing was bad. They weren't in the station yet, so he couldn't leave.

Ajay pushed through to the next car. He burst into a passenger car full of outrage and dismay. Half the people watched their screens in horror as their representative was shown to be a crook. The other half threw their hands up in rage and flooded the aisles.

The train howled its mighty whistle. They were close. Ajay's hack told him the conductor was upstairs, so he went down—directly into even more chaos.

"Computer guy!" Bernie blocked Ajay's escape and gestured at the tiny screen in his hand. "You did this?"

The car grew silent. Junior burst through the door. He was three steps out of reach of Ajay, but he stopped when he saw the looks on people's faces.

"It's deep fakes," said Junior.

"Maybe," Ajay said. He took a step forward. "But maybe it's believable enough. People have seen you, Junior. They know what you are deep down in their hearts. That instinct. The measure of a person that they get when they see a man use and abuse those around him. These people have it. Maybe they don't believe what they see on the screen. Lord knows the technology to make fake videos has far exceeded our ability to detect it. But nothing supersedes that sense people get deep down when they meet a man like you. It tells them to run. It tells them to beware of this man who could destroy them with a wave of his meaty fist."

"I could do that to you right now," Junior said. "I'll tear you apart and feed you to the dogs if you don't give back what you stole."

"Exactly as I'd expect you to," Ajay said. He drew the data chip from his pocket. "But, then, people wouldn't have access to the truth, would they? Hardware verified write-only data chip? This is what you really wanted from your father when you hired me. Not some stupid ring."

"I don't know what you're talking about."

"You didn't think I could figure out who was anonymously hiring thieves? The contract I showed your father was fake, but you wanted me to steal the ring."

"To test security," said Junior.

Ajay flipped the data chip and caught it. "What's on this, anyway? Money, of course. Vintage crypto is still worth a fortune on the collector's markets. The NFT images on this are worth more than your entire trust fund, aren't they?"

Junior looked around at the crowd. "He stole that from my father. He's nothing more than a thief."

Bernie spoke up, "I've never trusted a computer guy." He poked Ajay in the bruised ribs. "Especially not a guy like this. A hacker. They'll feed you a load of lies for breakfast, lunch, and dinner."

A slow smile crept over Junior's face.

The old man continued, holding up his screen, "But I believe this. He's right about this. I've known Junior Larrimer has been up to no good for years, and his father's worse." He stepped aside to let Ajay pass. "So, get out of here."

Junior opened his mouth to protest, but the crowd closed in on him. Ajay didn't wait around to see how it turned out. He turned to leave, winking at the old man as he passed.

"You owe me one, Ajay," the old man whispered.

"That I do, Bernie."

He pushed into the cargo cars, past the storage crates, and into the final car.

"Well," he said. The train was still moving, but it wasn't as fast as it was through Wisconsin. The Chicago portion of the trip dragged on as the train gradually slowed. "Let's see what we have here."

In the panel on the side of the drone, Ajay punched in the same code he'd seen Junior use on the screens in their private car.

It worked.

Ajay climbed into the drone car, activated the systems, and programmed his location. The top of the train opened, and the drone car unfolded upward, spinning up its rotors as it emerged from the speeding train.

He held the data chip in front of him as he lifted high into the air. This was the fortune he needed. It wouldn't be hard to convert into cash—

not on the vast online markets for such data. Once that was done, all he needed was a crew to pull off his heist.

As he flew past the Chicago skyline, he thought of the crew he would need. He thought of the skills that his people would have to have if they were going to have any chance at success—if his granddaughter was going to get the help she needed.

But that was a problem for another day.

PART 3

THE STATE FAIR AMBUSH

On a sweltering August afternoon, Ajay Andersen decided that the corner of Judson and Underwood, between the recently moved Union Hmong Kitchen and the accurately but not precisely named About a Foot Long Hot Dog, was as good a place as any to get shot.

Ajay clutched the head of his cane until his knobby knuckles turned white and watched the Minnesota State Fair flow like blood in a clotted vein through the streets of the state fairgrounds. He was a stone in the choked pulse of humanity, immovable in his patience.

The great Minnesotan get-together wasn't the kind of place he usually liked to be. For one, it was packed with people. Two hundred thousand human souls were expected to cram into the several blocks of the fairgrounds on the sunny Saturday. Most of them were the mass of humanity that Ajay in his old age had decided to avoid for various reasons.

A few of them were killers.

Ajay spotted her in the crowd several minutes before she bothered to come to their rendezvous. She wore a dark blue jumper over her wiry frame, aviator sunglasses to cover her dark eyes, and a black baseball cap over her long dark brown hair. Ajay's heart pounded in his chest when she glanced his direction, even though he knew that if he saw her, it was because she'd already decided not to kill him.

Chay Quinn was not the kind of woman to toy with her prey.

"I'm not here to lure you into a trap," Ajay said when she finally approached.

Chay looked at him down her long nose. "Really? Because you smell like bait."

"You know I wouldn't try anything against you."

"No, not like this," she agreed. "There must be a dozen cameras on this location, and half of Minnesota is casually strolling by at this very moment. You'd be a damn fool to try anything here."

"You know I own the cameras, Chay," said Ajay. As proof, he flashed the text up on the holographic display of his cane. The image showed the list of nearby cameras—not that Chay would understand what she was seeing.

"And I own half the crowd," said a man stepping from the flow of traffic. It was Olexie Sokolov, a Russian hacker and all-round asshole. He was a big man, nearly as old as Ajay, and if Ajay had to guess, the man's square jaw and square hair were made by the same chainsaw artist who had lined the fairground streets with blocky art. "So, we pretty much have it covered."

"Really," Chay deadpanned. "Half the crowd?"

"A significant percentage."

"Half?"

"Maybe three percent," Ajay said. "But it's enough."

"Three?" scoffed Olexie. "You underestimate me, American."

"Always have, always will," said Ajay, "but today I'm here to hire both of you."

Olexie's fingers danced over the controls of the fidget in his left hand. A holographic display showed a dozen social media accounts in a dozen different names. It *was* impressive. Olexie had done more in his career with Russia than Ajay would ever know.

Ajay gestured for the two to follow, joining the flow of the crowd as it moved up Underwood. "Word is Frontier Arms won't hire you anymore," he said to Chay.

"The separation was mutual," Chay said.

"Then they won't mind you taking this contract," said Ajay. She didn't respond, so he continued. "I have funding. I have information. All I need is a certain set of skills." He looked at each of them in turn. "You two have those skills."

"And it is nothing to do with Frontier Arms?" Olexie asked. "Because it would be bad if they were upset about something you were planning."

"Why do you say that?" asked Ajay.

Olexie held up his display. "Because they are here."

The image showed a large black camper surrounded by several men in black fatigues. A small tent in front of their rig offered pamphlets and recruitment paraphernalia. These mercenaries didn't carry visible firearms, but Ajay figured that was only because of their prominent location.

"Of course, they're here," said Ajay, not missing a beat. "They're one of Minnesota's biggest employers. It has nothing to do with us."

Olexie brought up another image. Three mercenaries made their way through the crowd, working their way south down Underwood. "Then why are three of them moving to surround us?"

Chay narrowed her eyes at Ajay. "What's this about, old man?"

"I didn't tip them off," Ajay said. "I swear."

Chay leaned so close Ajay could feel her hot breath on his face. "Is this supposed to be a test?"

Ajay reflexively took a step back, raising his hands. "I wouldn't do that to Gabby."

Chay stalked into the food building. A knife flashed in her hand, and Ajay didn't know where it had come from. He glanced at Olexie, who shrugged.

He needed Chay. He needed her trust and he needed her skills. Without her, there wasn't going to be a chance at what he needed to do, but if she suspected that he'd turned on her, she'd probably kill him, and that would be very bad for his granddaughter, Kylie.

Not so great for himself, either.

The smell of grease and salt and sugar assaulted his senses as he stepped into the building.

"I'm not going to forget this, Andersen," Chay shouted from across the small kitchen.

"Chay, wait," said Ajay. He brushed a protesting worker aside, and the man's hairnet bobbed in protest. "Wait!"

Chay turned. A knife flashed in her hand. To Ajay's surprise, a spark of desperation showed in the woman's dark eyes. "I never should have trusted you."

Ajay walked slowly forward, careful not to let his cane slip on the grease-slicked floor. "I was careful," Ajay said.

"Then it was that idiot," Chay said, tilting her chin toward Olexie, who had just entered the building. "He's given you up."

Ajay glanced back at Olexie. He needed the big man's skills, too, but gaining his trust wasn't exactly as important. "Maybe," Ajay said, "but we'll get out of this together."

Chay stepped closer to the door. "Not if they're onto us already."

An alert flashed on Ajay's cane and he glanced down at it. She was right. They surrounded the building, covering the exits.

"They won't be fully armed," Ajay said.

"Ha!" Olexie barked a laugh. He shoved a food worker aside. "They will have neuropellet guns and tasers."

"They can't—"

"Frontier Arms provides security here," said Olexie. "They get special rules."

Chay threw up her arms. "Great. You wanted to meet here because nobody can bring weapons here, but you forgot that the exact people we wanted to avoid are allowed to bring guns."

"Neuropellet guns," Olexie said.

"Neuropellet guns," Ajay agreed. "We can work with that."

"And what happens when they knock you out with a neuropellet?" Chay asked.

Again, Olexie laughed. "They drag you back to base and kill you! It is much better than being shot."

Ajay and Chay stared at the big Russian.

"Maybe it is *marginally* better." He checked an alert on his fidget. "But they are here, so we should discuss that with them."

"Three of us, three of them," said Chay. "I hope you two can fight."

Ajay blinked. "No, I—"

The door opened, and Chay Quinn moved like a cracked whip. She sprung forward as the thug led with his pistol, wrenched the weapon from his grasp, and fired a neuropellet into the underside of his chin. As he staggered backward, she turned and fired at Ajay—

Missing him by inches and striking the man entering from the other side of the building. The mercenary gasped in pain as the pellet struck the side of his temple.

The third attacker used the food window as cover, but Olexie saw him coming. He scooped a bucket of hot grease and splashed it over the counter. The man screamed and staggered away, to Olexie's great amusement.

"Let's move," said Ajay. He stepped to the side door where the mercenary still fought the effects of the neurotoxin.

"No!" Chay shouted, hand outstretched.

Ajay balked, and the door jamb in front of him exploded. He moved back into the building.

"They have covering support," Chay said. "These aren't idiots, you know."

She was right. Drone coverage. Maybe a sniper on a nearby building. They were trapped.

"Fuck, fuck, fuck," Chay swore. "Years of doing things right, and now one meeting with the legendary Grandfather Anonymous and suddenly my cover's blown." She stalked over to Ajay. The calm, collected, always-in-control killer he knew was gone. "This job better be as important as you said it was."

"It is," Ajay whispered. "For both of our girls."

"Give me one reason I shouldn't just leave you two idiots here."

The burned mercenary popped up in the window again, and Chay shot him in the face with her borrowed neuropellet gun.

Ajay drew a long, slow breath. He didn't *like* Chay. He didn't trust her. She was a killer, and she was possibly the most ruthless person he had ever met. Everyone would probably be better off if he let Frontier Arms take her down right there. She'd stop killing innocents. She'd stop fighting for the highest bidder. Everyone would be better off—except for Kylie.

And Gabby. Chay Quinn had taken custody of another girl like Ajay's granddaughter. A special girl, with abilities like almost nobody else in the world. The girls could interface directly with wireless computers, communicating with them as if it were their native language. But there was a danger to girls like that, and Ajay had learned of it in a previous job.

The Cascade. He still didn't know how it worked or what exactly it was, but it was responsible for the deaths of dozens of children. Ajay needed to know more about the Cascade, but for that, he needed the help of Chay and Olexie.

Ajay flashed through the camera coverage through the park. "Get me to the Frontier Arms mobile base," he said. "And I'll erase you from every Frontier Arms database on the planet."

Chay stared at him with cool, calculating eyes. Gone was the frazzled nerves and the trapped desperation. She was a killer again, and she knew what she had to do.

"No killing," Ajay said. "At all."

She hefted the gun in her hands. "I don't see how to get out of this building without dropping a few goons."

"I do," said Olexie. He already worked through his holographic display. Social media interfaces danced over his spotted old hands.

"What the hell good is that going to do?" Chay asked.

"Watch," said Ajay, stepping back.

Olexie worked for several long seconds, then grinned. "A hundred popular influencers think something is going to happen here very soon."

"What?" Chay asked.

"Put your gun away," said Ajay.

Reluctantly, Chay stashed the gun in her belt, covering it from view by untucking her shirt. It wasn't the best way to carry a weapon, but Ajay gave up on the idea of making her leave it behind. If he wanted her to avoid killing people, then the neuropellet pistol was the best thing for her to have.

"Stay calm," Olexie said.

The door burst open. Ajay could practically feel Chay's taut nerves. She was a spring ready to snap.

A dozen teenagers pushed into the building.

"Where is he?" asked one—the leader, obviously.

Olexie didn't miss a beat. He gestured to a closet door in the back of the building. "Sylvia Synth is busy at the moment."

"Who the hell are you?" the kid said to Olexie.

"None of your business."

The girl behind the teen whispered, "It's her manager." She showed an image of Olexie in a sharp suit at a table across from Sylvia Synth. The singer's trademark pink hair and wild makeup were toned down for the occasion, but it was clearly still her.

More teens arrived. Then more. Soon, the room was packed. When the building wouldn't hold any more people, Olexie gestured for Chay and Ajay to follow. "Keep your head down."

"That won't help against a decent drone," Ajay said. "Make sure to avoid walking the way you usually walk. They'll have gait detection activated. And if you look up even for a second, it'll spot you."

"Great," Chay drolled.

"And don't talk," said Ajay. He knew how drones found people in a crowd. He had designed the core systems for the NSA years ago, and technology had only advanced. His only hope was that the drones searching for them were only looking in the vicinity of the building.

They pushed through the crowd of gathering teens. Ajay was so out of touch with popular culture, he would not have heard of the wildly popular musician if not for Kylie. Sylvia Synth was the greatest musician since Prince, according to his granddaughter, and Minnesotans loved their musicians. Nobody in Minnesota got all that excited about movie stars or social media influencers. Musicians, though? Minnesotans had taste when it came to music.

And only Olexie had the tools to leverage that to his advantage. That was exactly why Ajay wanted the big Russian on his team.

They passed a mercenary on a bench. The welt under the man's chin was red and swollen, but he drew shallow breaths and looked as if he had simply sat down to take a break and fallen asleep. The neuropellets never worked as fast as bullets, but hit naked flesh and they *did* work reliably well.

Ajay, Chay, and Olexie stepped from the crowd of teens and into the surrounding throng of fairgoers. Ajay straightened his back, stepped with confidence, and led the two around the bend to the DNR building on Carnes Avenue. He tapped his cane, detaching his tiny drone and sending it high into the sky.

"We should leave," said Chay. "Break out while we can."

Ajay frowned at the video feed coming from his drone. "They'll expect that. They'll be watching all viable exits. What we need to do is— where did you get that?"

Olexie paused halfway through biting something fried on a stick. "It's a fried Snickers," he said. "You have to stick with the classics."

"Do you have to eat it *now?*"

"I'm blending in." Olexie took a bite of the cholesterol-filled mess. "And it's good."

Chay rolled her eyes. "I'm out."

"No, wait." Ajay put a hand on her shoulder as she walked away and instantly regretted it. She froze, and he could feel her coiled tension. "Gabby needs this, Chay."

"Don't you *dare* tell me what Gabby needs," Chay spat. "I know what you've done to your girl."

"Have you heard of the Cascade?"

"Guys," Olexie said through a mouthful of sugar.

Chay poked a finger at Ajay's chest. She had that desperate look in her eyes again. "*Your* girl has problems because *you* teach her to be weak."

"I teach her to care," Ajay said. "And she *is* kind. That's not what this is about."

"Guys," said Olexie again.

"Oh, you don't think so, huh? When you gaslight her until you can just push her around? I've watched you with her, Andersen. You're as over-bearing as any shitty dad."

Ajay blinked. He'd *been* a shitty dad. That wasn't how he was with Kylie. In fact, there was a good chance he was *too* permissive. He had let her go to a summer camp, even though he had reservations about it. He had watched her make her own mistakes and supported her when she needed help.

But he couldn't help who he was, and he was the kind of guy who saw the vulnerabilities in everything. He was a hacker, right down to the core of his being.

"Guys!" Olexie roared.

"What?" shouted Chay.

Olexie pointed down the street. "They're coming."

A pair of low-flying drones preceded the mercenary guards. Ajay watched as they made a tight scan of the street and set up a node in the perimeter around the exit. He had been right. There was no way they would get out without being spotted.

"They must know we're not in the food building anymore," Ajay said.

"Now what?" Chay asked. Her tone was accusing rather than questioning.

"Like I said." Ajay swept through the holographic controls of his cane until he showed the view his drone had picked up of the surrounding area. "We're one block from the base. If we can get in there, I'll be able to spike their data, giving us an opportunity to leave."

"And then what?"

"We'll deal with that when we get there," Ajay said. "But, Chay, you know I wouldn't have contacted you if this wasn't important."

"Says the man who lies for a living."

"*Lied*," Ajay said. "Past tense. I'm retired."

Chay stared at him for several long heartbeats, and Ajay got the distinct impression that he was being weighed. Crossing her arms, she said, "What's the plan?"

Ajay closed his eyes and drew a long, slow breath. He had never been much of a field agent. In his career with the NSA, he had always manipulated the world from behind a desk. Modern technology—the fall of cryptography in particular—meant that hackers needed to take a more hands-on approach to their work. They needed to interact with the world—to go *to* the problem and apply their wares. This was no different. The data node he needed to reach was protected by security guards.

"No killing," he said.

"It would only complicate matters," Chay agreed.

Olexie shrugged.

So Ajay told them his plan.

It started with Olexie and his social media manipulation. He already had an army of teens swarming an imaginary celebrity. All he needed was to move that group to the vicinity of the Frontier Arms mobile base.

But that took time. While he worked on that, Ajay set to cracking the difficult problem of disabling the drone surveillance. He couldn't hack them directly. They weren't receiving instructions from the ground but were rather flying with their own in-place AI, detecting dangers and flagging known enemies.

Ajay was a known enemy.

Hacking them wasn't possible. Shooting them wasn't practical. Ajay flew his one tiny drone across the vast open nothing above, searching for one of the primary surveillance drones.

Found it.

"They are coming," said Olexie once his mob was on the move. "But they are losing faith."

"Make it quick," said Ajay. He didn't know how long they would stay hidden.

Then, he found the drone. With a quick instruction sequence, he set his drone against it—not to bring it down, but to disable it in the simplest possible way: a flyby and a nice little spritz of paint.

"Done," he said.

"Done," said Olexie.

The crowd had swallowed them and was moving along Carnes toward the mobile base. Perfect.

Ajay slapped the big Russian on the back and said, "Be ready."

Then, he followed Chay.

The woman moved like a ghost through the heavy crowd. She never touched another soul, but she managed to pass through the dense clusters of humanity. Ajay grumpily elbowed his way through, following her lead as best he could. They started a block away from the mobile base, then they were half a block. The crowd flowed in the right direction, and soon Ajay realized that Chay was simply moving with the flow of traffic, but doing it in a way that nudged the flow where she wanted to go.

The mobile base was a modified black RV, with a satellite dish on top and an open operations center along the side. Half a dozen security guards lounged near a terminal, interacting with fairgoers and exuding low-grade menace into the otherwise festive atmosphere. When the crowd intensified, those security guards perked up to full alert.

Which was perfect.

"Six of them," Chay whispered.

"Is that a problem?"

"This whole day is a problem."

The guard closest to the terminal scanned through his feeds. He furrowed his brow when he saw the muddied video from the surveillance drones.

Full alert turned into something more. Now, hands were near weapons, and eyes were on the crowd.

Ajay stepped into the space between the flow of traffic and the mobile base. He leaned heavily on his cane. "Hello, gentlemen."

The lead security guard—a middle-aged man with a buzz cut and wraparound sunglasses—stared at Ajay. "It's the guy."

"Yeah, it is," said the man next to him. He reached for his neuro-pellet pistol.

"Ah, ah, guys." Ajay gestured at the crowd, many of whom were recording with their devices. "You have a PR directive, I'm sure. This is mostly a publicity event for Frontier Arms, right?"

The men grumbled, but they stepped forward to cut off Ajay's access to escape.

"Frontier wants to get away with as many murders as possible, and that means sending their least-competent idiots out to make them look like a legitimate company. A solid plan as long as those idiots aren't seen assaulting an innocent old man."

"We're not idiots," said one of the guards.

"That's up for debate," Ajay said.

"You're not innocent," said Buzzcut.

"No argument there, but they don't know that," Ajay said, indicating the crowd behind him. "Nothing gets social media shares like authority abusing its power in the state of Minnesota."

The guy chewed on that for a second. Ajay had their attention.

"Here's what I'm going to do," said Ajay, gripping the handle of his cane. "I'm going to walk over to that terminal over there. It's already unlocked using your biometrics, so I'd hardly even call it hacking to get access to the Frontier Arms central archives. I'm going to upload a piece of code that will erase me and my allies from your records. With any luck, it'll hit your backups as well. Frontier will still know I'm a threat, but they won't know why, and that works to my advantage just fine." Buzzcut tried to speak up, but Ajay continued, "Once that's finished, I'm going to purge all of your employment records. It'll be a great chance for you to pick up a new career. Maybe you can get a job shoveling manure or flipping burgers—you know, something befitting of your intelligence."

Buzzcut grabbed Ajay's arm with his big meaty fist. "Let's step inside and have a little chat," he said.

"Inside? Oh, that sounds much nicer. Better terminal access. Creature comforts. I assume your little RV has a foldout table like mine?"

The big guy yanked Ajay along so hard that he nearly lost his footing.

"Boss," said one of the other guys.

"Stay out here," said Buzzcut. "He's trying to distract us." He gave Ajay another pull. "And lock down that damn terminal."

The five guards scrambled to stand attention at their posts. One of them locked the terminal, returning it to a spinning Frontier Arms logo.

"Thanks for your help," said Ajay, earning himself another rough shove up into the mobile base. He scrambled forward and into the dark. Screens lined the walls, and a large weapons locker dominated one end of the vehicle. Ajay's eyes took a moment to adjust to the light.

Buzzcut closed the door behind him. "Now we can chat without any interference."

Ajay clicked the safety off on his cane's taser. He gripped it hard in his left hand, ready to strike as soon as Buzzcut came close. He would only have one chance. It needed to be a surprise.

It wasn't. He jabbed with the cane and Buzzcut batted it to the side. The big mercenary pounded Ajay with a boot like a block of iron. Ajay crumpled to the back of the RV, where the shadows were deepest. He clutched his chest and gasped for air. His cane was on the floor and his fingers ached from having it wrenched away.

"They told me all about you," said Buzzcut. "Warned me that you might be a problem."

"Did they warn you about the Russian?" Ajay said. His mouth tasted like lemons.

"He's just another damn hacker. Used to be a combatant. Not nearly as dangerous as you." He took a step forward, clearly enjoying the sense of his own menace in the enclosed space.

Ajay scrambled back until he hit the far wall of the RV. There was nowhere else to go. "But did they warn you about Chay Quinn?"

"Assassin. Lunatic. Yeah, we know about her."

"Do you know her real specialty?" Ajay asked. "The thing that makes her more dangerous than all of us combined? The thing that would let her easily take down those five guys you have outside the base or steal whatever's most valuable in this whole damn place?"

Buzzcut clenched his fists.

"I didn't think so, but I'll tell you." Ajay pulled himself to his feet. "Chay Quinn is good at sneaking into places undetected, especially when all the guards are busy paying attention to someone else. It's the reason you should worry about her."

"Why do you say that?"

Ajay let his focus slip from the big man to the space behind him, where Chay stepped from the shadows. His distraction had allowed her to sneak into the RV, and now all she needed to do was take out this one guy.

Without killing him.

Ajay's heart pounded. Chay was remorseless. Evil. Chay Quinn was the problem with the mercenary attitude. She defaulted toward violence and she'd never disable when killing was an option. It more than terrified Ajay. It left him in a moral quandary about using her skills at all.

But, she *did* have the skills he needed.

And this once—maybe *only* this once—she opted for the less violent path. She raised Ajay's cane and jabbed the taser end directly into the base of Buzzcut's skull. It crackled with electricity, and he went down hard. She was on him with zip ties, and by the time he had control of his jaw again, he was gagged and stuffed under a table.

"Do your thing," she said.

Ajay scanned Buzzcut's hand for a biometric login, bullied his way through layers of obfuscated data, and linked to the main Frontier Archives.

Because he hadn't lied. He did exactly as he said, purging Olexie, Chay, and himself from their databanks. It wouldn't stop the organization from tracking them, but it would make everything more difficult. Then, he found Buzzcut in the employee database—

And gave him a promotion and a raise.

"Let's go," he said.

"Where?" Chay asked. "There are still five guards outside"

A grin spread across Ajay's face.

Using his terminal access, Ajay tapped into the communication systems. He routed the video and audio feed through a system running on the core computer in his cane, adjusting the parameters so that it would use the recording that he had recently added to his archives.

"Team Alpha," he said, making his comm appear on the terminal on the outside of the mobile base. "Check in."

One of the guards scanned into the terminal. "All's clear out here," he said.

"Good," Ajay said. "Management wants this guy right away. Top priority."

The man on the video looked surprised.

"I know, I know. He's just an old man. But I'm driving him in."

"You're the boss," the guy said.

To Chay, Ajay said, "Drive, but take it slow."

She didn't move. "What did you just do?"

"Deep fake. They saw their boss on the video feed and they heard his voice. Even though everybody knows this technology exists, there are some situations where they just don't expect it. It doesn't even need to be very good, and they'll fall for it every time."

"That's... sobering."

The grin on Ajay's face threatened to split his face in half, not that he was so proud of his simple hack, but because he knew he had her. She now respected what he could do, and that's what it took to win her over to his side. They would still need to plan and execute their big job, but he now had the skills to get it done.

Chay pulled the mobile base out of its spot and drove it through the back exit of the fairgrounds, slowing only to pick up Olexie. It was a beast of a machine, and she had to drive extra slow to avoid the crowds. When they reached a light rail lot several miles away, Ajay had her park.

"You're not keeping this thing?"

"Nah," said Ajay. "I've got one of my own that I like better."

She watched him with her dark eyes, weighing him again. "You'll be in touch."

"I will."

With that, Chay Quinn disappeared. Ajay would call on her when he needed, confident that she would help.

"I don't like her," said Olexie.

"You don't have to like her, Olexie," said Ajay. "But I need her help."

"You will owe me drinks," Olexie said.

"I'll owe you money," Ajay said. "Also, you don't drink."

The big Russian grumbled all the way out the door. "Maybe I will if I need to work with that woman." Then, he, too, was gone.

Before he left, Ajay bent down to address the man with the buzz cut under the table. "You doing all right, Travis?"

The man nodded. When Ajay loosened his gag, Buzzcut said, "Your lady went a little tight with the zip ties."

"Need them loosened?"

"I'll live. My people will find me soon enough." His brow scrunched up. "Hey, how did you know she wouldn't kill me?"

"Oh, I didn't. That was why I needed this whole complicated setup."

Travis's eyes widened.

"I needed to know if I could trust her not to kill when the opportunity arose. If she did that on my real mission, she'd be endangering everything."

"That's dark, old man," said Travis.

"We do what we must," said Ajay. Just before stepping through the door, he turned back to the man. "The guys at the food building were a bit much."

A smile crept across the man's face. "Had to make things tough on you, didn't I?"

"That you did," he said. "That you did. Congrats on your promotion."

With that, Ajay left, crossed the parking lot to the light rail station and took the next train into Minneapolis.

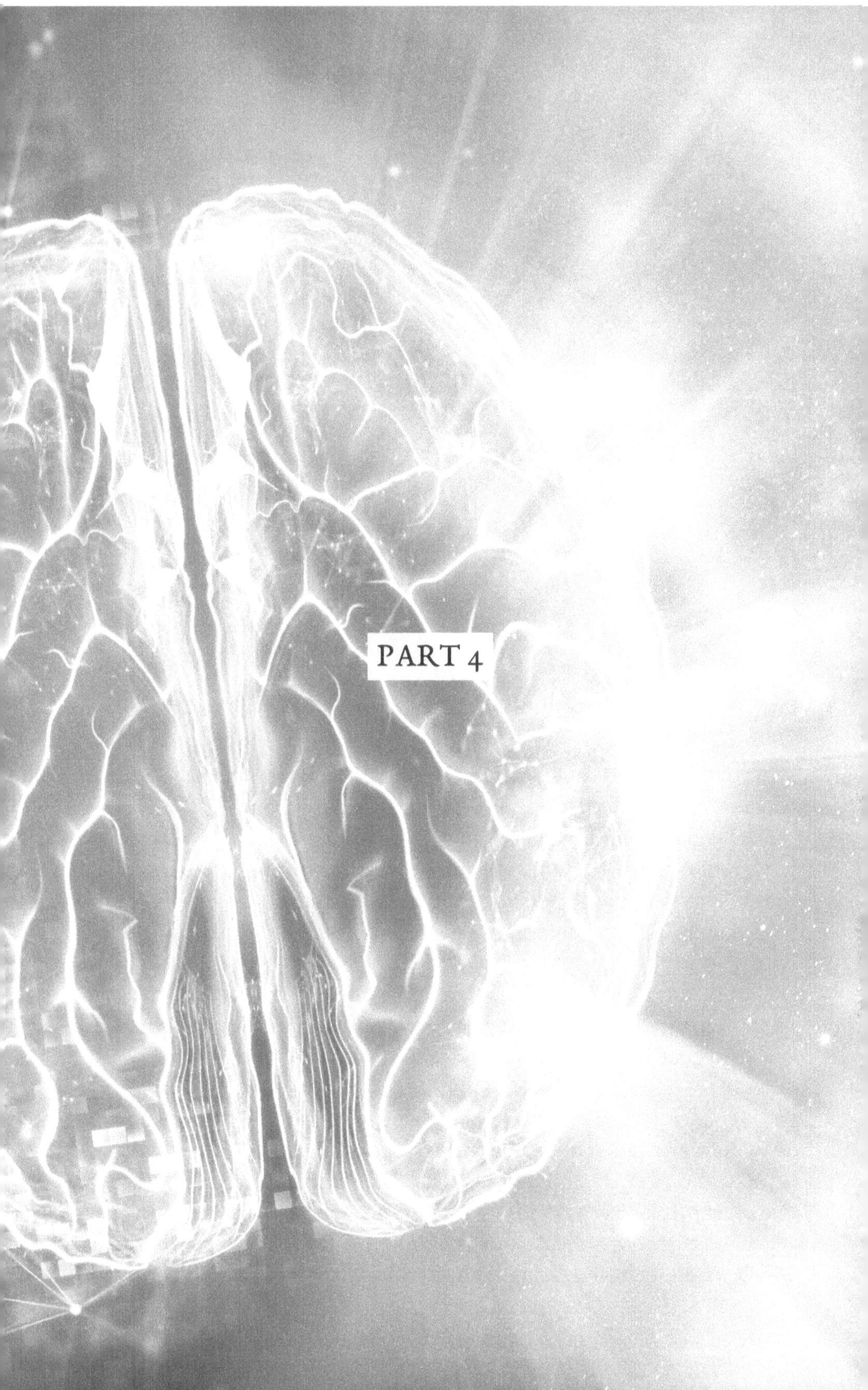
PART 4

INFILTRATION OF ELK RUN

"The Elk Run Biomedical Research Campus is the most secure biomed facility in all the Midwest, and Orin Instruments is its crown jewel," said Ajay Andersen. He gripped the handle of his umbrella so hard his knobby knuckles shook. He watched as the morning's workers disappeared into the dour facade past the acres of parking. "In the land of unlocked doors and friendly neighbors, this is a steel vault shrouded in barbed wire."

"Charming," rumbled Olexie. Ajay couldn't tell if the old Russian was serious or not. The big man had grown up in a place where bloc housing was de rigueur. The architecture the man appreciated was as gray and square as his head.

Chay Quinn stepped between the two men, whistling an awful asynchronous tune. She was a Lakota woman of average height, and the wry expression on her thin lips told Ajay that she was just barely tolerating the two older men. Chay was a killer. A professional. She had a knack for moving unseen through secure facilities. She continued her casual whistle, which was more intimidating than anything she could have said.

"You know I hate that song," Ajay said. It was one of Kylie's favorites. His granddaughter was the reason he was here, but it wasn't thanks to her awful taste in music.

Chay continued to whistle the trickiest sequence in the song, and a whisper of a smile slipped past her lips. "It's Gabby's favorite." Gabby was Chay's reason for being there.

"It's an earworm," Ajay grumbled. "I can feel it burrowing into my skull."

Chay poked a finger into Ajay's temple and gave him a shove. It hurt a little.

"All right then." Ajay did his best to ignore Chay, but when she started whistling again, he shushed her.

It wasn't raining enough for an umbrella, but it wasn't dry enough to go without. He used his as a makeshift cane as they crossed the expansive parking lot. Places like this in southern Minnesota always built out rather than up.

Ajay was the greatest hacker in the world, and here he was infiltrating the most secure biomed facility in the Midwest with nothing but an umbrella, a hearing aid, and his attitude. If there was something his India-born father and Norwegian-Minnesotan mother had in common, it was their capacity to be stubborn in the face of adversity.

Ajay gestured for Olexie to lead the way as they approached the building. "You're the expert, Mr. Sokolov."

"Anton Andrexi," Olexie introduced himself at the front desk. He gestured to Ajay and Chay. "These are my assistants, Boris and Amelia."

Ajay folded his hands over his makeshift cane and waited patiently. Olexie had used his connections to create the aliases for them. Ajay couldn't hack directly into the research conglomerate's network, but Olexie could manipulate the entire world around it. He produced false credentials and the research papers to back them up. He fooled professors at the University of Minnesota into thinking they'd had decades-long relationships with a Russian scientist named Anton Andrexi. He had circulated rumors that Andrexi had solved the problem of neuroplastic adaptation in newly augmented brains.

It was technology that was critical to Ajay's granddaughter Kylie and Chay's ward Gabby. Such technology could solve the Cascade, which had killed so many other children with similar neurological augments.

Olexie was a social hacker, and Ajay only hoped the big man's skills at deception would work as well in person as they did online.

The lure was something Elk Run's leader, Genevieve Polard, couldn't possibly resist, cobbled together from information Ajay had stolen from a dying man—one of the inventors of the biomedical technology Elk Run had built its empire on. The preliminary work for this job had cost a fortune, from buying access to groundbreaking research to influencing pillars of the scientific community to manufacturing the illusion of legitimacy. Not even to mention buying and programming the drone that was soaring high above Elk Run in a holding pattern.

It surprised Ajay, however, when Polard herself stepped into the lobby. A bronze band held back her silver hair, and the icy blue of her eyes caught the turquoise of the tinted lobby windows. She wasn't a tall woman, but she walked with such authority that she might as well have towered over them all.

Genevieve shook Olexie's hand. "A pleasure, Mr. Andrexi."

"The pleasure is all mine," purred the Russian in an awful fake accent somewhere between German and Spanish.

"Come," Genevieve beckoned, after superficially acknowledging Chay and Ajay. "I'll give you the tour, and then my engineers are excited to hear about your research."

"A tour from the bigwig herself," murmured Ajay to Chay as they fell in step behind Olexie and Genevieve.

"No reason to make things easy, right?"

A pair of security guards watched as they each stepped through a full-body scanner. Once they had all been cleared, they stepped into a second lobby made of brutal corners softened only by fake plants. A single high window shone hazy gray light onto rows of hard benches.

Olexie's job had been to peel back the first layer of security, but he had done it too well. He'd impressed the researchers so much they'd sent the CEO for a personal tour. A CEO wasn't going to be lax in security, abandoning Chay and Ajay to do what they needed. A CEO would never—

"Why don't you two wait here," said Genevieve. "I'd like to show Mr. Andrexi some of our latest advancements in the lab, but I'm afraid our security team only gave him the high-level clearance required."

"No problem," said Ajay. Was it really going to be this easy? "We'll wait right here."

Chay had the wherewithal to look mildly offended. "We were told we'd get the full lab tour."

Genevieve's lip twisted. "We will summon you if the security team clears your background check."

Chay wasn't having it. "We're supposed to stay with—"

"I'll be fine, dear," said Olexie. A hint of a quaver slipped into his voice, making him sound very old. Vulnerable. He turned to Ajay. "I promise I won't reveal any of our research."

Ajay folded both hands atop his umbrella and considered Chay and Olexie. "We will wait."

Olexie and Genevieve disappeared into the complex.

"You have to put up a fight," Chay explained. "I mean, we came all this way, right?"

"I suppose."

"We're not supposed to be fine with sitting here in the lobby."

"No, that makes sense."

"They think that you're here to keep the big guy from spilling confidential data," Chay said. "That's why they want to separate us."

Which was fine because they wanted to be separated. "I'm better with computers."

She narrowed her eyes at him. "You just don't like conflict."

The lobby was quiet and sterile, like the lifeless halls of an underfunded nursing home. The decorative light in the adjacent alcoves flickered, but Ajay sat with his back straight and his expression bland. Nobody else came through security. Nobody came to tell them that they'd been cleared to see the rest of the building. Nobody appeared to be watching. Somebody was definitely watching.

Chay whispered through the side of her mouth, "I'm tired of being on camera."

"I count three," Ajay said.

"Five. You missed the one in the fake plant and the one in the thermostat."

"No, I counted the one in the thermostat," said Ajay. Five cameras. That was a lot, even if he had the proper tools, which he did not. He was starting to doubt his ability to reach the Orin databanks. "Oh. I missed the obvious one on the ceiling."

"That one's a decoy," said Chay. "The most important part of sneaking around is knowing where the eyes are, old man."

"And ears."

"Yeah. That's harder. Still got that song in your head?"

Yes. "No."

"Are you ready to move?"

No. "Yes." Ajay stood from the bench and tapped his umbrella on the floor. Playing up his limp somewhat, he made his way down the hall to the courtyard.

"Excuse me, sir?" called the receptionist as she rounded the corner. She had been watching.

He ignored her. The bathrooms were only a dozen paces away according to the blueprints he'd studied. That would be his best shot at a camera dead zone. If he could just—

"Excuse me!" she called again. The clop of her flat shoes resonated on the polished white floor. "Sir?"

He needed more distance. A few more steps. He almost reached the door when he felt the woman's firm grip on his shoulder. His umbrella clicked on the floor in the rhythm of that awful song. Dammit, he hated async synth pop.

"Sir, I'm going to have to ask you to..." She trailed off when she saw his expression.

He gestured palms upraised in the universal question and pointed to his ear where his hearing aid was visible. "It's not working," he shouted, taking another step down the hall. The receptionist wasn't quite out of the angle of the camera in the fake plant.

Chay signaled for him to keep going. A few more steps and he would be in the blind spot.

The receptionist's grip tightened. "I'm going to have to ask you to return to your seat."

Again, Ajay pointed to his hearing aid.

She pointed at the bench, surprised when she found Chay had walked up behind her.

Chay took the pointing hand, locked the elbow, and shoved the woman into the restroom. Before the door swung shut, Chay slammed the woman to the floor and pressed a knife to her neck.

"No killing," Ajay hissed.

Then the door swung closed. Ajay waited for the span of several rapid heartbeats, then continued down the hall. Chay knew her part. He only had to trust that she wouldn't kill anyone.

He didn't trust her at all, but there wasn't much he could do about it.

Ajay passed a conference room with two glass walls and an enormous screen. Olexie stood in the front of the room, gesticulating wildly at the complex diagrams depicting their false data while a dozen men and women watched with blank faces.

The courtyard sat in the center of the complex and was filled with young oaks yellow with fall color. The courtyard was locked, of course, but it was only locked to prevent entrance from outdoors. Ajay pushed his way through, opening his umbrella as he stepped into the cool mist. He kicked a rock into the doorway to prop it open and strolled along the short path nestled into the manicured landscape.

The path created an illusion of seclusion, with plants that obscured views in strategic ways to give the impression of distance from the structured world of the biomed complex that surrounded it. Ajay walked slowly, his hip bothered him when he wasn't using a cane, but he could endure for as long as it would take.

It didn't take long.

Security wouldn't let him bring tech through the door. He was lucky to enter with his hearing aid. The umbrella wasn't tech, though. It was a harmless umbrella with a big rainbow target on top. A rainbow target that would be easily spotted by the drone flying above.

Something struck his umbrella with a snap and tumbled to the ground. Ajay swept it up and made for the courtyard door.

"You get it?" Chay asked.

Ajay held up the piece. It was a glasses case with a small inscription on the side. One end tapered into a universal data port key. "The receptionist?"

"Handled."

"Killed?"

Chay shot him a dirty look.

"Let's go."

Peel the onion. The biomed center's security was built in layers. The front door was the outermost shell. The cameras and sensors in the halls were another layer. That got them inside, but it didn't get them where they needed to be. Each layer had its own solution, and Ajay needed to get to the innermost layer where the most vital data was stored.

Olexie was the solution to the first layer. Chay the solution to the second. As they made their way through the narrow hallways built like a rat maze in an especially bland science experiment, Chay kept note of every sensor and camera they ran into. Some, she disabled. Others, she circumvented. A wall panel opened, taking them into an office. Another time, they dodged a sensor array by moving through a drop ceiling.

This is what she was good at. This is what she was the best at.

Ajay opened the case and removed a pair of thin, half-moon glasses. His reading cheaters didn't just help him read small text. They would automatically connect to nearby wireless devices using a routine he programmed himself.

Because even the most serious companies had flaws in their security. The Elk Run Biomedical Center had cut corners with software updates. Orin Instruments had budgets to maintain. The hacks he had spent weeks writing were able to bend the network to his will. After several minutes and a dozen quick detours, the camera network was his.

After that, it was only a matter of accessing the internal site map—there were changes he hadn't seen on the blueprints. Changes that any reputable biomed company would want to keep secret.

A pair of wiry engineers approached, but Ajay saw them in his coopted video feed. He redirected Chay to another branch of the maze. "It's down," said Ajay. "Three levels."

"We're on the ground floor."

"Sometimes we find unexpected layers."

"And sometimes things are exactly as they seem." She glanced up at the ceiling. "I'll stick to my end of the deal. You stick to yours." With that, Chay stood on a desk, popped the ceiling panel out of place, and disappeared into the darkness above.

Layers, layers, layers. He spent thirty of his precious remaining seconds studying the maps to find a path down to the layers below. Almost the entire floor down below was left off of the records. Nothing on the network mentioned its existence, except for a single line in the security protocol that demanded increased permissions for anyone attempting to reach that level.

If higher permissions were what he needed, then higher permissions he would have, because that was what he was good at.

He stepped out of the office and walked slowly down the corridor using his umbrella as a cane. He reached a small lobby with a single elevator. His glasses detected the signal coming from a security panel but failed to connect.

"Must be on the right track," he said. "Security's getting tighter."

But not tight enough. Ajay took the case from his pocket. He pressed it against the reader panel and used his glasses to scan the field for vulnerabilities. Seconds passed. His heart pounded. The air was dry and cold in the office portion of the complex, and his lungs ached.

A yellow alert in the corner of his glasses indicated that someone was approaching. Ajay glanced at the thin video feed and saw Olexie being led by Genevieve and a cluster of engineers. He furiously ran through a series of low-level hacks, scouring the machine code for known flaws. Maybe they wouldn't come this way.

The alert flared red as the group rounded a corner. They were approaching fast, and Ajay didn't think there was anything else in this wing of the complex. His wireless connection forced a key exchange, and Ajay pushed a bogus key into the elevator's wireless module and recorded the data it sent with the rejection. If he could decode that data—if there was a vulnerability in what it sent...

They would arrive in seconds. He wasn't going to make it. The elevator was the toughest security they'd hit so far, and it was the kind of hack that might take him weeks. Why hadn't his research turned up this possibility?

The panel beeped. The elevator opened.

Without looking, Ajay stepped inside, opening his umbrella to block the view of the camera inside. He pressed the case against the panel inside and waited for the computer inside to sync with the controls. After several more seconds, he had what he needed.

Access. The elevator closed and descended.

"Easy," he muttered to himself. "Too easy."

The elevator's screen displayed B3 and the door opened.

Ajay felt like he had stepped into a hospital. His umbrella clacked against linoleum floors and the lights in the ceiling rained down a white light so harsh it felt like it shone right through his thin, brown skin. Somewhere, machines beeped with insistent urgency, and a clatter of tools rang down the hall. A gurney stood askew against the far wall, its sheets decorated with an ominous brown stain, but all Ajay could smell was the sharp bite of disinfectant.

Focus. He needed information on the Cascade, and if it was killing children, this might be the place to find it. He should have expected every horror a corporate machine might throw at him. He made his way down the long hall, stopping at each open door to peer inside. He didn't find any banks of computers. His glasses detected no signals save the one now ascending away in the elevator.

Double doors ahead of him burst open, and a pair of men in scrubs pushed a gurney through. Ajay's heart slammed in his chest. He stumbled backward, reached out a hand, and stepped through the first open door he found.

A human body lay on a stainless steel table. A child, not more than ten. His covered body was held in stasis by the cool, dry air, and the unmistakable scent of formaldehyde seeped into Ajay's pores.

One stainless steel wall contained a dozen oversized drawers. Ajay, heart pounding, touched one of them with the end of his cane. Did he dare open this?

He thought of Kylie, with all her passion for life. What would he do if she were taken from him like this? All at once, he despised the people who would do this. He hated them for it. He wanted to burn the entire Elk Run Biomed Research Center to the ground.

"Are you here for Jonas?" asked a voice behind him.

Ajay turned to see a man in a lab coat leaning against the wall. "Um, yes, of course."

The man stepped forward with a quirk of a smile. He motioned for Ajay to follow and led him all the way to the end of the hall. Through another pair of double doors, the hall looked not like a hospital, but like any apartment anywhere in the world. There was worn brown Berber carpet, warm hallway lights, and numbers on each door. The man in the lab coat brought him to the last door on the end: door 313. "He's been expecting you."

Layers. Like an onion, sometimes layers of security go soft. Ajay had found the slimy core of this onion, and suddenly there was no more resistance. He drew a long breath. Now that he was there, he didn't look forward to the next step.

He took it anyway. Opening the gray door, he entered.

Into a room of vivid colors and insipid background music. The carpet was a pattern of roads and buildings: the map of a fictional city. The walls were bright blue with streaks of green and pink. One wall was a mural of a fantasy landscape complete with castle and mountains.

In the center of the room was a rocking chair, and in that chair rocked a slender child not much older than the boy in the morgue.

"I know why you're here," said the boy. He was slender and blond, and his hazel eyes pierced Ajay's soul.

"Why am I here?" Ajay asked, closing the door behind him. Across the room, there was an open doorway that led to a little kitchenette and a hallway that stretched into the darkness. "Why are you here?"

"I live here," said the boy. He smiled with his lips, but there was nothing like a laugh in his eyes. Something about how the boy's hazel eyes danced while he talked didn't seem right. Like he was a blind man casting around for the stimulation of light. "They don't like it when I know things."

Ajay stepped forward. "What kinds of things do you know?"

The boy rocked slowly in the chair. "I don't think I recognize you."

Ajay's feet pressed fresh footprints into the otherwise unmarred carpet. The boy's eyes didn't follow, but Ajay got the distinct impression of being watched. He looked to the corners of the ceiling but didn't spot the hidden cameras that must have been there.

"They don't like it when we look for the cameras," said the boy.

"Cameras are expensive to replace." Especially the kind that could see through walls. The room was a perfect replica of a happy family's home, even if the boy wasn't normal by any stretch of the imagination.

"All of my brothers are dead," said the boy. "They went through that door."

"That man said your name was Jonas?"

The boy nodded.

"It was you, wasn't it?" Ajay asked. "The elevator. The cameras in the hallway."

"They don't like us messing with the cameras."

"No, but you did anyway. You pointed them the other way so that I didn't get caught. This place has more surveillance than a Silicon Valley startup. You see everything that happens here."

Jonas closed his eyes and drew a long, slow breath.

There was something wrong about this place—something wrong with Jonas and the way his stolid expression played on his young face. Something wrong with this room and the dark hallway that led deeper into a gloomy apartment. There was, of course, something wrong with keeping a boy like this hidden below ground for his whole life, but that didn't surprise Ajay.

His granddaughter had suffered a similar fate for the first decade of her life. How many more facilities like this had popped up using similar technology? Biotech had been used to successfully modify this boy's brain as it developed. He would one day be in the same situation as Kylie.

If he survived.

"What can you tell me about the Cascade?" Ajay asked.

The boy twitched.

Ajay moved around Jonas toward the hallway.

"I wouldn't go down there if I were you."

Seconds ticked by. How much longer did Ajay have before he needed to escape? Could he possibly take this boy with him? Those scientists outside the room may have let Ajay enter without contest, but they would stop the boy if he attempted to leave.

"I have to see," Ajay said.

When the boy didn't answer, Ajay moved down the hall. His umbrella tapped on the thin carpet, and he breathed the dry air. Above, a single bar of light flickered like failing fluorescent lights. Its arrhythmic strobe imposed its juttering tension on Ajay's nerves. He passed closed doors on either side, but ahead, once he was in the long hallway, he saw what he wanted.

The static on the screen resembled a dead channel on an old CRT. A keyboard sat recessed in the wall underneath, but Ajay didn't need that. He found the data port in a hidden panel to one side. His glasses still didn't pick up a wireless signal.

"You won't like it," said Jonas.

Ajay jumped. Jonas was right behind him in the flickering dark hall. The boy stood almost as tall as Ajay, his slender form inconsistent in the unsteady light.

"They never do," the boy said.

Ajay plugged into the data port, and text flew across his thin glasses. The stream of information was too much to read in a hundred lifetimes, but as soon as it started to flow, a piece of code kicked in and short text summaries started to appear.

"The Cascade," Ajay said. "What is it?" He didn't know if he was talking to the boy or the program sorting through the data.

"It's almost got me," said the boy.

"Then why don't you tell me what it is, and I'll try to help."

The boy took a step back.

Ajay quickly read the summary that cast itself onto his retinas. The Cascade was a sequence of information that led to eventual catastrophic information collapse and death. For people like Jonas, thinking about the Cascade caused the Cascade. Thinking about avoiding the Cascade caused the Cascade. It was a logical loop that their brains could not avoid because their brains were part machine.

He looked Jonas in the eyes and opened his mouth to say something—but what could he say? Light flickered across the boy's glassy gaze. "How are you still alive?"

There had been others like Kylie. Others who had never survived the long, difficult journey to adulthood. The pursuit of this technology had never been legal or in any way ethical, but its failure rate was what stunted the program's reach. If this Cascade was to blame—was it something that could still affect his granddaughter?

Seconds ticked away. If Ajay didn't meet Chay and Olexie at the designated time, he would need to find his own way out.

The data flow stopped. He had what he needed from the inner vault. Ajay stowed the glasses case in his pocket and said, "Tell me what you know about the Cascade."

"No."

The screen at the end of the hall flickered, and an image of Olexie appeared. He stood across a steel table from Genevieve, whose scowl could have peeled paint.

"You are responsible." Olexie's shout was tinny and strange through the room's speakers. "If you could not solve this, you should not have started this project."

Genevieve jabbed a perfectly manicured nail at the big Russian. "You lied to us."

It was falling apart, Ajay realized, and fast. He needed to leave before Olexie revealed everything.

Ajay couldn't hear what happened next, but Olexie and Genevieve covered their ears and shied away from some unseen speaker.

"What's happening?" Ajay asked.

Then, Chay appeared on the screen. A view down a long hallway showed her dropping from the ceiling and entering the room. She snapped a kick out at Genevieve, catching her in the jaw. Chay grabbed Olexie and pulled him away. The two ran down the hall, but another view opened, showing the security guards closing in fast.

"I get it," said Ajay. "You don't want to talk about the Cascade."

The screen flickered and the boy glared at Ajay. "I don't think about it."

"People talk without thinking all the time."

"The thought unmakes us," said Jonas.

"Yes, but what is the thought?" He had to know more. Kylie was vulnerable to the Cascade, and if he didn't understand it, he'd never be able to protect her.

Jonas' eyes glazed over and he stood in the flickering light. On the video, Olexie and Chay fought a pair of guards. Chay took the taser from one and used it on the other. Olexie heaved a large desk in front of a door, trapping them in an office.

"There must be a way around it," Ajay said.

Jonas said, "It is the end thought, and every time I think it, that part of my mind must disappear."

Dammit. Ajay wasn't getting anywhere. He gestured in front of his glasses enough to trigger a search of the data he had downloaded. "What triggers the Cascade?"

Nothing. The researchers didn't know.

On the screen, Olexie slammed a chair into the tinted office window. It bounced off, leaving a tiny crack.

The screen returned to a static haze.

"It can't be stopped," Jonas said. "It can't be fixed."

Ajay placed a hand on the boy's shoulder. "Listen to me, Jonas. Tell me everything you know."

The screen flared to life, showing the people in the hospital outside his little home. They worked tirelessly on their experiments. Their pace was frantic. Their sunken eyes and pale skin told of too many hours searching for an answer.

The answer to the Cascade.

He needed to go. Olexie and Chay were in bad shape, but it wasn't too late. They could still escape. Everything they had done—every minute they spent preparing for this raid on Elk Run—had been for a singular purpose. Ever since he had found that single line referencing the Cascade, he had known he needed this. He had the data, so it was time to run.

But he couldn't leave this kid.

Then, it started to all make sense. "You didn't just help me once I was here," Ajay said. "You sent me the tip about Randall Bent's data brick. You gave me the clues that I needed to find this place." He remembered what Jonas had said about the others not liking what they found about the Cascade. "And you've done it before."

Jonas sat in his rocking chair and stared at the screen. The image changed, and Olexie burst through the office window just as the guards broke in. He leaped out, followed by Chay, but they weren't on an outer wall. Ajay recognized the trees of the courtyard.

They weren't on the first floor, either. The view switched, and Ajay watched as Olexie hit the soft earth of the courtyard and collapsed. Chay landed in a roll, ready to take on whatever came.

"You have to help me," the boy said.

"You've cut out parts of your own mind to stop it. Emotion. Empathy. You've crippled your own ability to think in an effort to excavate it from your brain, but you're still thinking it, aren't you?"

"No!" The boy clutched his fingers together.

On the screen, Olexie burst up as more guards swarmed into the courtyard. The old Russian slammed one guard to the side and disarmed the other with one fluid movement. With a mighty heave, he wrenched a bench out of the ground and swung it.

Beside him, Chay fought a man twice her size. Every time he swung his taser, she dipped to the side, luring him along.

All the while, she whistled.

"It's an earworm," said Ajay. "It's the song you can't get out of your head and it's made a thousand times worse because you know that you die when the music stops. Of course, you can't get rid of it. Who could ever forget something like that?"

The boy clutched his head. "It's always there. It goes and goes and it never stops."

"All this time you've been resisting, but resisting only makes it stronger. You've had the best neurologists in here to help. The best psychologists. The best chemists looking for the imbalance in your brain." Ajay knelt next to the boy and placed a hand on his shoulder. "None of it works, and that's why you came to me."

"The best hacker."

Ajay couldn't resist the smile that crossed his lips. He had once been the best hacker. Maybe he wasn't anymore, but he knew how machines worked.

This boy was no machine. Not as much as the kid imagined, anyway.

Olexie looked to the skies. Above, the leaves on the trees whipped around from a sudden wind.

"Your drone is here, but they won't escape unless I let them," said the boy. His whole body trembled.

"Then let them."

"Not until—"

The claws of Ajay's bony fingers dug into the boy's back. He didn't like being threatened. When he spoke again, it was with the authority granted him by the accumulation of his years. "Let. Them. Go."

More guards burst into the courtyard. Chay moved like lightning. A strike to a neck. A twist and a throw. One was disarmed, and she held the gun to his head. A tense breath passed. Olexie shouted.

Chay fired the gun.

Stillness.

Ajay swallowed his own horror. He had worked with killers before. He had seen the dark in their eyes as they killed in combat and cold blood. Ajay had told Chay not to kill anyone. He had stipulated from the very beginning that she was, under no circumstances, to murder anyone. Not in the heat of combat. Not in cold blood. Not even if she hated them with all her heart.

But ultimately, he had brought her there. He was responsible for everything she did on this mission, and his actions had just resulted in—

In—

The guard held up his hands. Tears rolled down his cheeks. She hadn't shot him in the head. She had fired the gun into the wall next to him.

And now it was a hostage situation, except the boy didn't care at all for the hostages.

"Give me a command window," said Ajay, stepping up to the screen. A box appeared over the video feed with a text prompt.

Ajay fell into the hack. He wouldn't typically attempt something without hundreds of hours of preparation. His handy utilities and pre-programmed tools would almost always give him the advantage he needed. Hacking, after all, wasn't about cleverness. It was about preparedness. It was about knowing the target and understanding its potential weaknesses.

But this—this was a test of cleverness. The window was access to the boy's brain, where the tools were organically grown and the rules were often nonsensical. Ajay probed the edges of his access. He found the parts of the boy's mind that had been sequestered away.

There was so much of it. The boy he met was only a tiny fraction of the fully functional being. Who would he be once he was set free? How dangerous would this make him?

He found the Cascade as well. It lived in those darkened spaces as a self-replicating monstrosity of code that danced equally from brain to machine. It grew and occupied every space it touched, and its precursors lived even in the brightest spaces in the boy's mind. There was no removing it. Nothing Ajay did could purge this code.

In the video, Olexie shouted at Chay, who calmly held a gun to the guard's head. They were in the center of the courtyard. Above, Ajay's extraction drone roared above the rooftops. More guards surrounded them. The standoff dripped tension, made even more intense by the lack of sound.

Sound.

He stopped and took a step back from the screen, watching the data flow for several long seconds. The saccharine elevator music played over unseen speakers.

"You can't hear," he said.

"I can."

"No. This isn't the same." He cast around for a camera. "You're reading lips. You're using sensors in the walls to replicate hearing. In fact, you've rebuilt almost the entire sense using tools that are not connected to your ears, but it's not hearing. Not quite." He swiped through the controls again, looking for the specific connections. There! "The first thing you disabled in your brain was the part of you that processes sound. That's where your problem is. To fix this, you're going to need to hear again."

The boy stood. Ajay didn't turn to look at him, but in the reflection on the screen, he could see the boy's brows knit in anger. "You're like the rest."

"No," said Ajay, still furiously swiping through the controls. The boy was closing off his access as quickly as he could think, but Ajay used what he had to reopen his connections. He only needed to stay in for a little longer. "I'm not like the others."

"They said to ignore it and it would go away. You're no different!" His fists were clenched at his sides. His face was going red. "I can't just ignore it!"

Another closed connection. Ajay swiped through a routine and reopened it. He needed to make progress, but it was all he could do to fight Jonas. On the screen, three more guards swarmed in from the other side of the courtyard, with Genevieve on their heels.

"Trust me," Ajay whispered. His lips hardly moved when he said it again. "Trust me."

The boy froze. Ajay could feel the tension in the boy's body as he strained to understand.

Again, Ajay whispered, moving his lips even less, "You have to trust me if you're going to survive, Jonas. You're going to have to trust someone."

Jonas didn't open the connection to the part of his brain that processed hearing, but he thought about it. In thinking, the machine parts of his brain probed the right data space. Ajay grabbed that stream and filed them away.

"You're stuck, Jonas," Ajay said. "Stuck because no new sound can enter, meaning that the earworm digging its way through your brain will only continue to echo until it reaches every part of your mind. The only way to fix that is to give it something new."

"No," said Jonas, more weakly than before.

"It'll work, Jonas." Ajay queued up several small routines. He furiously coded one final piece. "You have to trust me."

On the screen, the guards advanced. Chay had a chance. She could have shot her hostage, if even to wound him.

But she didn't. After a brief struggle, the guards slammed Olexie into the dirt. Chay dropped her weapon and raised her hands, defeated.

Ajay finished his code. "There's a difference between me and all the psychologists and neurologists you've met."

"You're a hacker and you can force these changes," said Jonas, finally resigned to his fate.

"No," said Ajay, smashing the button to engage his sequence of routines. "I'm the grandparent of a teenage girl."

The program unlocked the boy's brain. Every tagged blockade fell in a flash, flooding his mind with the toppling cascade of doom. Whatever it was—whatever hooks the suicidal ideation had—burrowed deeper into his skull. They seized the myriad functions of his hybrid neurological structure and threatened to cause the whole thing to seize.

But it didn't stand a chance, because the final piece clicked into place. Kylie's favorite song—the synth-pop monstrosity that had plagued Ajay's life for weeks—thundered through the room.

Jonas froze. For a moment, Ajay thought it might be a seizure. Maybe his plan hadn't worked, and the boy was nearing the end.

Then, as Sylvia Synth's high-pitched vocals crashed into a rolling, asynchronous rhythm, the boy's head started to bob. His eyes lit up, and a smile crossed his face.

On the screen, Ajay monitored the progress of the horrid synth pop as it overwhelmed the boy's Cascade. The dark tendrils of blocked code shook loose one by one, not fully disappearing, but failing to congeal into a dangerous worm.

When the song finished, Ajay closed his window. On the screen, he saw Olexie and Chay being escorted through the halls.

"Let us go," Ajay said.

The boy's eyes sparkled. "You beat the Cascade."

Ajay walked to the door. At first, he had thought of rescuing the kid—breaking him out of this prison. But it wasn't a prison. This was home. Jonas was in control here more than anyone else.

"Stay in touch, kid," Ajay said as he left. "And let me know if you ever need another visit."

As he left, the thundering synth pop rattled the walls of the boy's little home. When he passed the scientists, they all looked up.

Then, the boy appeared in the door behind him. The scientists must have read the expression on his face because they started to clap. Ajay ignored them, umbrella clacking on the linoleum floor. Guards met him when the elevator opened on the first level, and they escorted him outside to the parking lot, where he met with Olexie and Chay.

"They let us go?" Olexie mused as they climbed into the car.

"Negotiations can happen when you refrain from killing needlessly," said Ajay.

"That's never been my experience," said Chay.

Ajay gripped the handle of his umbrella. "Well, maybe we can just chalk this up as an anomaly."

"Did you get what we needed?" Chay asked after they had been on the highway for several minutes.

"I did."

"And?"

"You should let Gabby listen to whatever music she likes," said Ajay. "Even if it's awful."

With that, they drove north, surrounded by brilliant autumn color. Ajay finally felt that he understood the rumored Cascade. It wouldn't be a threat to Kylie, and Chay would be able to keep Gabby safe. He wondered if unethical biomed experiments around the country might use what he discovered to expand their efforts, but he couldn't spend time worrying about that. If they did use what he learned, they would only be using it to save children who would otherwise die from the cascade.

His work had saved those children.

He only had to hope that it didn't also revive the dying industry.

But that was a problem for another day.

VULNERABIL
Locked
HOLOOFOA

STOP
DANGER!
Locked

AFTERWORD

"Old people can't be good at computers."

It's one of the most common complaints I see for my Old Code series, and I'm not afraid to say it's a load of crap. My father, an old person, is one of the most brilliant guys I know when it comes to computer hardware. He's been repairing computers for fun and profit (he's mostly paid in cookies these days) for something around forty years. Is he familiar with the most modern technologies regarding AI or quantum computing? Well, no. But he's extremely competent in the areas of technology that interest him. That's hardware, ham radio, and certain kinds of strategy video games.

People don't get dumb when they get old. They just don't. In a certain number of years, I will be an old person. I expect to still be pretty good at the parts of tech that interest me.

That'll be AI and maybe a little quantum computing. I'll probably never be as good as my dad at fixing hardware.

"People can't function through that much pain."

Another common complaint about these books, but this one's totally fair. The kind of abuse Ajay struggles through borders on ridiculous.

But, look. You never met my grandpa. Grandpa Eichenlaub once shattered his collarbone while on a canoing trip. Rather than stop and get a ride home, he decided to just tough it out for miles of tough rapids, tricky bends, and tons of active rowing. Why? Oh, it didn't hurt that bad.

It did, Grandpa. It had to.

But he continued, anyway. Sometimes people are stubborn like that.

"It's too fast paced."

Fair enough. When I was writing this, my goal was—

"It's too slow paced."

Oh, come on.

Anyway, I hope you've enjoyed these four connected short stories. I've presented them here today as a novella, but really they were originally written to be serialized as four separate episodes. That project fell through, but I'm really happy that I was able to bring these to you.

If you have any complaints, or, god forbid, compliments, I'd be thrilled to see a review on this or any of my books. Reviews are the absolute best and easiest way to help an author do what they love to do.

More by Anthony W. Eichenlaub

Old Code
Grandfather Anonymous
Grandfather Ghost
Grandfather Guardian
Grandfather Zero
Grandfather Crypto

Colony of Edge
Of a Strange World Made
Upon Another Edge Broken
On a Forsaken Land Found
From a Barren Seed Grown
Above a Distant Sky Seen

Metal and Men
Justice in an Age of Metal and Men
Peace in an Age of Metal and Men
Honor in an Age of Metal and Men

www.ingramcontent.com/pod-product-compliance
Lightning Source LLC
Chambersburg PA
CBHW061503210726
48287CB00007B/2634